PENGUIN BOOKS

RISING REIGN

Tessa Hale, author of love stories with magic, usually with more than one love interest. Constant daydreamer.

Also by Tessa Hale

The Wolves of Crescent Creek series

Crescent Kingdom

Eclipsed Empire

Rising Reign

RISING REIGN

TESSA HALE

PENGUIN BOOKS

PENGUIN BOOKS

UK | USA | Canada | Ireland | Australia
India | New Zealand | South Africa

Penguin Books is part of the Penguin Random House group of companies
whose addresses can be found at global.penguinrandomhouse.com

Penguin Random House UK,
One Embassy Gardens, 8 Viaduct Gardens, London SW11 7BW
penguin.co.uk

Penguin Random House UK

First published in the US by Bloom Books 2026
Published in Penguin Books 2026
001

Printed and bound in Great Britain by Clays Ltd, Elcograf S.p.A.

The authorised representative in the EEA is Penguin Random House Ireland,
Morrison Chambers, 32 Nassau Street, Dublin D02 YH68

A CIP catalogue record for this book is available from the British Library

ISBN: 978-1-807-83053-3

Penguin Random House is committed to a sustainable future
for our business, our readers and our planet. This book is made
from Forest Stewardship Council® certified paper.

FSC www.fsc.org MIX Paper FSC® C018179

CHAPTER ONE

Wren

RAIN PELTED MY SKIN, FEELING LIKE TINY KNIVES SLICING into me. But, still, I tipped my face to the darkening sky. *Water.* I needed this water. Opening my mouth, I caught as many drops on my tongue as possible.

I kept my eyes closed. It was easier that way, trying not to take in the surrounding walls of the pit. The towering way they enclosed me. The occasional snake that made its way down. The countless creepy-crawlies.

Breathe, Wren.

I forced my inhale to slow. No jerky, stuttered breaths that would feed my panic. As I brought the muggy air into my lungs, I scented the bayou water—the thick heaviness of it—and the rotting aromas that seemed to cling to my father's territory.

No. Not my father. Bastian. The bastard who'd taken everything from me.

My back screamed, and the memories of the whip slicing into

my flesh rose. A lash for every month I'd been away. My wolf pressed at my skin, wanting out, wanting to rid the world of every being who had caused us harm.

"With time," I whispered. "With time."

I lifted the shirt that had been given to me after the lashing, letting out a whimper as it peeled away from my blood-caked skin. Keeping my eyes closed, I called on my wolf—not for a full transition, but enough to bring on some healing.

My skin tingled as I felt fur ripple over my limbs, torso, and then my face. My breaths turned into those short pants I was trying to hold off—pain-filled ones—as my knees finally gave way, and I hit the muddy ground with a thud.

The healing was necessary but took far too much energy. Especially when I hadn't been given food or water in at least seventy-two hours. As my fingers dug into the mud, I pictured the guys in my mind. I painted each of their faces in such detail that it felt like I could reach out and touch each one.

A keening noise left my lips, my wolf crying out at being separated from her mates. My human half was just as devastated. Everything in me ached, and it was from more than just the beatings I'd taken. It was a soul-deep pain.

But I kept breathing. For the guys and for myself. I refused to let Bastian Boudreaux win. He wouldn't break me.

I slowly forced my eyes open. It was getting darker, ramping the panic inside me higher. But then I pictured Locke—the way he held me and soothed my touch-hunger, how his voice sounded with his gentle reassurances—and the panic eased a fraction.

Leaning back on my heels, I studied my surroundings: mud and stone held in place by what looked like heavy-duty chicken wire or something similar. It was the only thing keeping the pit from collapsing since it was so close to the water.

The rain eased a bit, but as it did, a shiver racked me. *Not a good sign.* My shifter nature should've protected me from the cold. If it wasn't, my energy stores were running on empty.

I didn't let the fear of that realization in. I let logic reign. Because Bastian didn't want me dead. Not yet, anyway. He wanted me to feel every ounce of pain that he and his minions dished out.

A shudder ran through me at the memory of Marcelle's snarling face as he took his turn with the whip. The way he'd grabbed my hair afterward and whispered, *"Just wait until you're in heat. I'm going to make you pay in ways your nightmares can't even imagine."*

Breathe, Wren. Just breathe.

This time, I pictured Kingston. The way his callused hands felt as they framed my face. How he promised that everything would be okay and made it so. The sweet, thoughtful gifts he left for me to find.

My panic eased again. Because the guys were my talismans, my guiding lights. And I would find my way back to them.

Footsteps sounded in the distance, and I instantly launched to my feet, every muscle and limb crying out in protest. I might've healed myself, but that sort of pain lived on like an echo you couldn't wash away.

I tipped my head back, watching, waiting, listening. The steps were heavy, likely male, and carried anger.

Steeling myself, I tapped into my empath gift ever so slightly.

Pure darkness slammed into me, making me stumble. I instantly threw up my walls, but the darkness still slid inside. Nausea rolled through me as sheer agony raged.

Then, a face appeared over the side of the pit, and Marcelle sneered. "Enjoying being back where you belong, bitch?"

I struggled to pull air into my lungs. The rotting bayou scents of the Red River and Marcelle's stomach-turning stench filled my nose.

"Nothing to say?" he snarled. "Good. I like my women silent and obedient. You'll be trained as such."

I nearly vomited then but managed to keep a hold of myself. Losing any water from my system now could be catastrophic.

Marcelle threw a rope ladder down, and I scurried to get out of its path.

"That's it. Run, little bitch."

I bit the inside of my cheek to hold back my retort as the ladder clattered against the side of the pit.

"Start climbing. Your father wants to see you."

It took everything in me to hold back my shudder. I didn't want to give Marcelle or Bastian the satisfaction. Instead, I began to climb.

I'd tried refusing as a child, curled into a ball at the bottom of the pit, and hoping for death. Instead, I'd gotten the worst beating of my life. Then Bastian had brought a healer to fix me, only to do it all over again. I'd learned to never refuse.

But something about choosing to climb to my own punishment was even more painful. It made me feel weak and pathetic.

"You're strong," I whispered to myself. "You survive. That's what matters."

"What'd you say, little bitch?" Marcelle snapped.

I didn't answer. Instead, I pictured Brix in my mind. The way he'd shielded himself and his emotions for so long. How strong he'd been through his pain. And the way he'd let me in—the gift that was. If he could make it through, so could I.

My entire body cried out in pain as I climbed. Muscle. Skin. Bones. Everything felt like it was a second away from irrevocably breaking.

"Faster," Marcelle demanded.

I tried. My muscles screamed, but I pushed harder. The second I was within arm's reach, he grabbed me by the hair, dragged me out, and threw me to the ground. I slid through the mud like some disgusting Slip 'N Slide.

Marcelle's nose flared. "You stink."

No shit, Sherlock.

I refrained from giving voice to that thought. But whose fault was it that I smelled? It wasn't as if they'd given me access to a shower.

"Get up," he barked.

I struggled to my feet, my muscles quaking.

Marcelle was on me in two long strides, grabbing me by the hair again. "Start walking."

I did as I was ordered. The pit was on the outskirts of the pack territory, with small cabins belonging to the lowest-ranking members surrounding it. Bastian didn't want to listen to his prisoners scream all night long.

As Marcelle marched me along, a few people poked their heads out of their houses, curious to see the alpha's traitorous daughter. There was a mix of reactions. Those loyal to my father sneered and spat. Others looked fearful. And a few looked sad—one or two even angry.

Something pricked my awareness: the realization that none of the women wore shoes. My stomach cramped. I didn't have shoes on either. I never did on pack territory because my father thought it would keep me from running. But now, *none* of the women were allowed?

Marcelle's lip curled as he followed my line of sight. "*You* cost them that privilege. You, and you alone. They all despise you."

My shoulders curled in as if wings could spring from my back and protect me from the onslaught of the words. It did no good. The knowledge that the women of this pack were being hurt because of me sliced me to my bones.

"Keep it moving," Marcelle said, shoving me forward by my head.

I stumbled, my feet sticking in the mud, but I kept moving. I took in the cabins through the mossy trees. They got nicer and larger the closer we got to the main house—Bastian's home. It loomed in the distance.

It stuck out like a sore thumb against the more rustic cabins: white paint and columns that gleamed amid the swampy backdrop.

It didn't fit. Just like my father didn't—fake and not true to its nature.

But Marcelle didn't guide me toward it. Instead, he turned me. That's when I saw them—torches lighting the darkening sky and forming a circle.

That twisting sensation was back in my stomach for a whole new reason now.

Two massive bonfires roared on either side of the circle, with a dais of sorts behind it. A chair like a throne loomed highest, snarling wolves carved into the posts and battle scenes playing out on the legs as my father sat impassively atop it, a woman kneeling at his feet.

I lifted my chin, refusing to be cowed by his flair for the dramatic. I would meet whatever he had planned head-on. I would not cower.

Marcelle shoved me toward the dais. I stumbled, but I didn't fall.

Bastian's gaze skimmed over me. "Little Flower, you're looking a little worse for wear."

I didn't make a sound; just stared at him.

His lips twitched. "Such defiance in you. Such fire. It's surprising, really. Maybe there is hope for the line that comes from you yet. But you'll have to prove yourself."

Marcelle scoffed, but I pretended I couldn't hear.

Bastian's fingers drummed on the arm of his chair, his many rings glittering in the firelight. "If you succeed, you'll receive a shower, a meal, and a bed for the night. If you fail, it's back to the pit for another week."

I didn't let hope show on my face. It would bring Bastian too much pleasure.

"But you'll have to win it," he growled.

Dread pooled low in my stomach. *Win it.*

I knew what that meant. The torches. The bonfires. The gathering pack.

They lived for these nights—the bloody battles that entertained Bastian and could earn them favor for a fleeting moment. But I was a submissive, and the past three days of torment had left me weak, my strength fleeting.

Bastian reached out a hand to grab the kneeling woman's chin and lifted it. "Tell me, pet. Will you fight for my honor?"

"Yes, Alpha," she whispered demurely. But I saw her muscles ripple as she spoke. Everything about her was a finely honed machine.

"Rise, Lilli," Bastian commanded.

She did so gracefully, and my mouth went dry. The woman had at least a foot on me, and as she stretched, I saw that I'd been right about that muscle. The scars across her knuckles told me she was no stranger to a fight.

Bastian leveled his stare at me. "You will fight for the privilege of my shelter. You will fight until death itself comes knocking."

CHAPTER TWO

Kingston

I stared into the fire as it crackled. It should've been too warm to have one, but the Colorado mountains had turned bitterly cold surprisingly early this year—as if the mountains, too, were grieving the loss of Wren, crying out for her return. My wolf howled inside me, raging against the walls I'd constructed around him.

There was no way I could set him free right now. I didn't trust him not to turn feral and run straight for Louisiana. He'd head right to Wren and get us all killed in the process.

The pacing footsteps behind me grated, with their panicked quickness and desperate back-and-forth. I didn't think Puck had stopped moving since Wren disappeared. "We need to move," he growled.

I didn't turn; I just kept staring into the fire as if it held all the answers in the world. "We need a plan. We need to know for sure if Wren is on pack territory, and we need reinforcements."

To anyone else, my voice would sound as if it held no emotion at all. Only I knew that each word was filled with agony. Failure. Guilt. Emotional destruction of the highest order.

The clicking sound intensified, spurred on by my words. "I'm trying," Locke growled. "Their system is good, but if I can hack into their security cameras, I'll at least know what we're walking into."

After the fire, we'd tracked the Red River wolves to the airstrip north of town. But that's where their scents—and Wren's—had disappeared. Locke had done his thing and hacked into the flight records. They'd tried to cover their tracks by flying to Texas and then Kentucky, but the private plane's final destination had been a small town several hours outside New Orleans. I knew in my bones that Bastian had taken her back to Red River.

A fresh wave of agony slammed into me. Wren, at the hands of a monster, the same man who had done such damage to my sister that she'd taken her life. My mind couldn't help but invent the worst images of Wren enduring all that and more.

My fingers tightened around the edge of the stone fireplace mantel. A crack sounded, and the rock beneath my hand crumbled to dust.

A palm landed on my shoulder, fingers squeezing. I knew by scent that it was the one person I least expected, Brix, the man Wren had healed in untold ways. Someone who'd been so averse to any touch that wasn't painful now sought to comfort me.

"It's not your fault," he whispered.

I shoved out of his hold and stalked away. Puck may have had it right with all the pacing. "Ender, anything from your source?"

He shook his head, his expression completely impassive. "He's pulling all his usual lines. I'll hear back as soon as he has something."

Fuck.

Every second we did nothing was another that Wren lived in agony. My vision went blurry as fury surged. I moved without thinking, letting out a roar as I grabbed the antique coffee table and hurled it at the wall.

It splintered into countless pieces, shattering glasses of drinks and plates of uneaten food with it. The whole room went silent. The only sounds were the pieces of my destruction settling and the fire's crackles and pops.

My chest heaved as I dragged in ragged breaths. It wasn't enough. Nothing was. I'd failed Wren in the worst possible way, and now she was paying the price.

I charged toward the hutch against the wall, needing to shatter that, too. Puck, Brix, and Ender all moved in, Brix and Ender grabbing my arms as I battled against them, snarling and snapping.

"Fuck," Puck muttered. "Should I get a tranq?"

We kept them in the medical room in case one of us slipped into a feral state, but the idea of him injecting me with one now only had me fighting harder.

Ender cursed. "Yes. Get it. Now!"

"Wait!" Locke yelled. "I'm in."

Those two words ignited the barest amount of hope in me. A lead. Information. Something that could help us get Wren back safely.

The urge to fight slid clean out of me. Brix and Ender kept a hold of me, waiting to see if it was a false submission, but it wasn't. After a few seconds, they released me.

I scrubbed a hand over my face. "I'm sorry. I—"

"Bugger off," Puck muttered. "I hated that table anyway."

I wanted to laugh, but I couldn't make the sound. Instead, I rounded the couch, wanting to see the computer. The others followed. Locke's fingers alternated between typing and using the trackpad. And then they stilled altogether.

"Fucking hell," he swore, then expanded a camera view.

Wren stood before Bastian, who was on a goddamned throne, but that wasn't what had Locke panicking. It was Wren's back. She faced away from the camera, which had to be tucked in a tree, and wore an oversized T-shirt that should've been white, given the color of the sleeves. Instead, it was stained pink, red, and brown, with a mixture of blood and mud.

Wren's scars played in my mind. Evidence of all the torture she'd endured at her father's hand. And now she was back there. My back teeth gnashed so hard I was fairly certain I'd fractured a molar. But I didn't give a damn. I only had eyes for Wren.

"We have to get her out," Puck rasped. "We can't leave her there."

Brix's breaths came quicker, more ragged. "I…am going… to kill…each and every one of them. I am going to bathe in their blood and put their heads on pikes."

"Locke," Ender said, his voice devoid of all emotion. "Map out every camera location and watchpoint." He looked at me. "They're right. We can't wait any longer."

I knew he was right. It didn't matter that we were up against a pack thirty times the size of ours. We'd find a way. "I'll ready the plane."

My phone rang as I pulled it out, but the sound was a notification for the gate. I frowned and tapped the screen. A familiar face poked out of an SUV window and filled my screen. "Hera? What are you doing here?"

Her pale-green eyes were hard as she stared back at me. "I know how to get her back."

CHAPTER THREE

Wren

A FIST SLAMMED INTO MY FACE, MAKING MY HEAD SNAP back, but I barely felt the pain. I was numb to it now, and that was for the best.

The past forty-eight hours had been challenge after challenge, my father losing more and more patience as I defeated each of his female wolves. The first had been his *pet*, a woman who, even now, glared at me from her spot at his feet. Next had been one of his female enforcers. Next, I was going up against one of the *male* enforcers.

The males of our species had more strength—it was a physical-makeup thing—but that didn't matter when I could use their size against them. Especially after my father had been forced to make good on his word to give me a hot meal, a shower, and a bed for the night. My strength had been revitalized.

The problem was, he hadn't been foolish enough to make any

promises since. I'd gotten one cup of water between bouts today and had been forced to sleep in the pit again. But he wouldn't break me.

When I summoned one of the guys in my mind again, it was Ender this time, his hard expression telling me I was better than this. His words lashed out, demanding that I finish the asshole. I called on his strength and cunning.

I ducked impossibly low as the enforcer's leg struck out in a snap kick. When he reached the height of his kick, I rushed in. Lightning-fast, I grabbed his foot and forced him to his back. He landed with a thud, mud flying everywhere.

I didn't lose my momentum. I moved in and wrapped my arms and legs around him in a triangle choke. His fingers lengthened to claws—a dirty move since shifting was prohibited in these matches—and he raked them down my sides and legs.

I couldn't help but cry out as someone in the crowd booed and another cheered. But I held on through it all. The enforcer's face grew redder, and I felt him fading. Another one, two, three, and the man collapsed on me altogether.

I shoved him off the moment he did and clambered to my feet. My chest heaved, each inhale making my sides scream in pain where the deepest gouges were. I tried to mentally assess my energy stores to see if I had enough to heal myself, but I wasn't sure I did. Especially not if Bastian planned to send me into another fight.

The only sign of anger in Bastian's face was the slight twitch of muscle next to his mouth. "Is my pack truly *this* pathetic? No one can best my *submissive* bitch of a hybrid daughter? She's an abomination!"

None of his words hit like they had as a child. Because I now knew them for the lies they were.

A mountain of a man stepped forward. I didn't recognize him from my childhood, meaning he must be new to the pack and *chose* to become part of Red River. Which meant he liked the darkness residing here.

"I will best her, Alpha. I will honor you," the man growled.

He had to weigh three times what I did, and I swore the ground trembled as he stepped forward.

A smile curved Bastian's mouth. "I knew I could count on you, Rex."

"I'm not sure that's the best idea, Bastian," a new voice said. It was smoky but with a hint of warmth. I couldn't see the woman's face because she wore a cape with a hood that covered her head.

A few growls and snarls lit the air, but Bastian held up a hand to silence them. "Speak, healer."

The woman slowly pushed back her cowl and revealed beautiful, strawberry-blond hair and stunning, pale-green eyes. Her skin was like porcelain, dusted with freckles across her nose. No part of her looked like she belonged here.

The woman smiled, and I swore the tension swirling in the air eased a fraction. "Thank you, Alpha. If you wish your daughter to carry any young, you must not put her through these trials. If you keep putting this type of stress on her, her wolf will never allow her heat to come."

I stilled, no longer feeling peace at the woman's presence. I wanted to rip her throat out. A female wolf's heat came once a year, but if a wolf were starved or in some extreme distress, it wouldn't come upon her at all. I was glad as hell for that fact currently.

Bastian's eyes narrowed on me. I was sure he was taking in my shabby state and more than just the mud covering most of me. I had a black eye, a split lip, and was now bleeding everywhere, thanks to the enforcer's claws.

"Lilli, clean her up," Bastian ordered. "Then I want the healer to examine her."

Bastian's pet cast angry eyes up at him. "But, Bas—"

He slapped her so hard that she flew off the dais and landed in the mud. "You will show me respect."

The woman trembled, her eyes downcast. "I'm sorry, Alpha."

"Do as I said," he barked.

I wasn't sure what would've been worse: being escorted by

Lilli or Marcelle. But given that a shower was likely, I'd take Lilli every time.

The she-wolf pushed to her feet, stalked over to me, and grabbed my arm, letting her claws out so they pierced my muscle. I swallowed back a cry, refusing to let her win.

Lilli dragged me toward the house as Bastian called for two more fighters, his bloodlust evidently not satiated by my bouts. "You're going to pay for that, bitch."

I kept my thoughts and words to myself, not missing that the healer followed quietly behind us. Lilli hauled me up the stairs and into the room I'd stayed in the night before—the one that had been mine in my early childhood.

There was a mural on the wall of a wolf in a field of wildflowers and a canopy bed fit for the princess Bastian had hoped I'd be until he found out about my submissive nature. It was too much on top of my tainted blood.

Lilli shoved me, making me stumble. "Clean yourself up, bitch."

As she stalked off, the caped woman stepped inside the bedroom and closed the door behind her. I bared my teeth. "You even *think* about doing some hocus pocus to make my heat come on, and I will rip out your throat."

The woman smiled at me as if she felt genuine joy from my words. "Good." Then she slipped a hand into her pocket. She fished out a tiny drawstring bag and emptied what looked like a powder into her hand.

I started to back away, looking for a weapon in the room, but the healer was faster. She whispered an incantation and then blew the powder toward me. "Remember, Wren. Remember."

The moment the particles and spell hit me, so did the memories. It was as if I was watching the events from above: the guys standing around me in the medical room, my body shredded. I recognized the clothing. It was the same as I'd been wearing when the Death Walkers took me. This woman was there, too.

The so-called memories came in flashes, snatches of a few seconds of a reel, but one thing was clear. This woman had been… healing me. She must have been the one who'd saved me when I was close to death. The one I'd never met in a conscious state.

I jerked myself out of the spell-induced haze and stumbled back a step. "You healed me," I rasped.

She placed a finger to her lips, and I knew why. Listening ears could be anywhere. "Hera. Nice to meet you officially."

I blinked and mouthed, "*What are you doing here?*"

"There'll be time for that later. First, let's get you cleaned up."

Hera pulled out another pouch and rolled it between her hands as she chanted. She moved closer, pouring the contents over my head as she continued her incantation. The herbs swirled around me, lighting in the air until they slammed into me all at once.

I sucked in a breath. It didn't hurt, exactly. It felt more like someone had injected me with pure adrenaline. My heart raced, and my pulse thrummed. Everything sped up to superspeed around me. And then it all just…stopped.

Time froze for a count of three and then returned to normal. I looked down at myself. The mud and blood were gone, along with the injuries. I felt…good. *More* than good. I felt the strongest I had in months.

"W-what did you do?" I stammered.

"What Bastian asked." She tapped her ear to indicate that someone was listening. "I healed you." She slowly strode across the room, pressed something into my hand, and leaned in. "Be ready."

A moment later, she was gone, the door closing and locking behind her. I slowly uncurled my fingers and found a knife. One I recognized. One that made my eyes sting as I read the single word etched into the handle.

KINGSTON.

CHAPTER FOUR

Wren

MUSIC BLARED FROM SOMEWHERE OUTSIDE, CARRYING with it the sounds of drunken revelry. It took a lot of alcohol to get a wolf shifter drunk, but the Red River pack was always up for the challenge. Bastian's bloodlust must have been satiated by whoever battled after me, turning him on to different entertainment.

I lay on the bed, knowing I should try to sleep but terrified to shut my eyes. Hera's words echoed over and over in my mind. *"Be ready."*

I was scared to let hope find a home in my chest. Afraid to believe the guys might be planning some sort of rescue mission. Just thinking about it had fear grabbing hold. The Arcane pack had five wolves. Red River consisted of almost one hundred now. It was no contest. The guys would be slaughtered.

Everything in me twisted, pulling taut. I couldn't be

responsible for something happening to them. Couldn't handle a world without them in it.

My door swung open, and I leapt to my feet. The knife Hera had given me—tucked into my side beneath the jeans someone had laid out for me—flared hot with my awareness of it. But I didn't reach for it. Not even when Marcelle strode into the room.

His upper lip curled. "Your father wants you at the party."

I didn't say anything. Figured that was my only weapon at the moment. But I braced, ready if Marcelle made a wrong move.

He grabbed my arm and hauled me downstairs. "Bastian thinks that healer knows all, but I think we could beat you bloody, and you could carry my young all the same."

I did everything I could not to shiver as nausea rolled through me at his words.

Marcelle waited for me to say something, anything. When I didn't, he let out a low growl and dragged me outside. "I'll be hearing you scream in no time."

His words sliced through the loud country music, and I knew they'd live in my nightmares forever. Marcelle hauled me through the crowd as people danced and drank. Couples made out or ground against each other—a few were even having sex out in the open.

Bastian sat on the dais again, watching it all, Lilli at his side and Hera hovering nearby. My stomach flipped. I wanted to believe I could trust her, but trust didn't come easily to someone like me.

Marcelle continued shoving me through the crowd until we reached something that hadn't been there earlier. A fucking cage. He grinned at me. "Your father wants you here, but he's not taking any chances this time. Get inside."

I didn't move at first, still too shocked by the metal bars that looked like something from the Middle Ages.

Marcelle hauled open the door and shoved me inside, then turned the lock and pocketed the key. "I'll be seeing you, *Little Flower.*"

The music got impossibly louder, making my ears ache. The other wolves here likely didn't care because of their drunken states. Bastian seemed unaffected by it; he simply sat and watched the debauchery play out in front of him like his favorite show. Bastian loved two things: pleasure and pain.

At times, I wasn't sure which he enjoyed more. But looking at him now, I knew it was pain. He looked on as his wolves drank, danced, and rutted, but he didn't enjoy any of it as much as he did the brutal fights.

Movement caught my eye, and I managed to duck at the last possible moment as a bottle flew at my head.

"Might be a traitorous bitch, but she's fast," a man I vaguely recognized slurred.

Bastian cackled. I knew the sound so well that I could pick it out through the music and voices. Pleasure in others' pain. That made him the happiest.

"Cunt," a woman accused, throwing whatever was in her cup at me.

Some sort of red punch splashed over me, sticky and smelling sweet with a hint of alcohol. I gnashed my back molars, and my knife burned a hole in my side. My fingers itched to pull it free.

"Traitor!" a man yelled, hurling something at my cage. I managed to duck again, realizing it was a fucking rock.

Bastian howled with laughter. "Tell me, healer. Could you cure someone with a hole in their head?"

Hera's lips thinned. "That steps too far."

"Pity," Bastian muttered. "I'd so enjoy seeing it."

A familiar whizzing sound pricked my ears—something so faint I almost missed it. And then they fell. The man who'd thrown the beer bottle. The woman with the fruit punch. The man with the rock.

They all collapsed to the ground, arrows sticking from their chests.

My gaze flew to the trees, the only place the projectiles could've come from, and I thought only one word: *Ender.*

Chaos erupted. Enforcers raced for my father, moving to get him into the house, and he ran like the coward he was. But only after barking orders at everyone else.

Other Red River pack members began to fall, but only the ones taking up fighting positions. Many of the wolves simply fled because they had no true loyalty to Bastian.

The mountain man who'd offered to fight me shifted into an equally massive brown-and-gray wolf and ran for the trees. My stomach sank at the thought of him going up against one of the guys. They'd be okay. They had to be.

Sounds of fighting past where I could see erupted, and the panic dug in. A familiar wolf with piercing green eyes ran at a Red River man, pointing a gun at the tree line. Puck leapt into the air, grabbed the man by the neck, and shook him like a rag doll. A second later, the man fell, his eyes vacant as blood dripped from Puck's mouth.

Movement flashed in my peripheral vision. Another familiar figure emerged, but this one had dread pooling low in my gut. Marcelle prowled toward my cage.

"You think you're going to get free, little bitch?" He slid a key into the lock and jerked open the door. He was fast—so fast I had no chance to block him. The blow to my cheek had me staggering back, and then he grabbed me by the throat. "I'll kill you before I see you free."

"No," I wheezed. "I'll kill *you*."

I grabbed the knife from my waistband, flipped it open, and shoved the blade deep into Marcelle's chest. His eyes went wide with shock, and his grip on me loosened. And then he fell. I kept a hold of the knife as he crumpled to the ground. Blood seeped through the material of his shirt and spilled onto the dirt beneath him.

Dead. I'd killed him.

CHAPTER FIVE

Brix

I RAN THROUGH THE FOREST, MY WOLF'S VISION TAKING OVER as my four paws hit the ground at record speed. The only thing I could think of was Wren. It didn't matter how much care we'd put into our planning; this could go wrong in many ways—especially because the sheer size of the Red River territory meant we each had to enter alone.

We had our pack link to keep us in contact, but no one was watching our backs. Ender had said it was the only way. We needed to take out the enforcers on patrol first.

It was lucky the Red River pack had a watchtower system. Their guards stayed high in those towers except for during their hourly patrols. Locke had watched the feeds to figure out the timing, and we'd struck just as they were all climbing down.

But the moment Ender started taking the bastards out with arrows, all hell broke loose. My brothers needed backup, and they needed it now.

I pressed harder, my muscles aching as I ran for where Ender had said Wren was being held. Puck was already there, and Locke and King were on their way.

Wren.

An image of her played in my mind. The way her eyes lit when I revealed the tattoo I'd inked into her skin. The tender way she looked at me when it was just the two of us. How she eased everything inside me.

A snarl lit the air. My hackles rose just as a brown-and-gray wolf slammed into me. We rolled as he took me down, but I used his size against him, letting his weight pull him to the bottom position.

I snapped at his neck as he raked his claws across my gut. Pain bloomed, but I ignored it, moving to bite him again. He dodged, gouging my shoulder with his claws, but it left him exposed. I managed to get his neck this time and didn't hold back.

My teeth sank into his fur, and I tore out his jugular. His blood tasted...wrong. Drugs, I realized. I spat it out as the wolf's eyes went wide and then stilled, unblinking. Just one more black mark on my soul. But worth it to get Wren free.

I tore through the woods again as Ender's voice filled my mind. *Hurry, he's got her, and I don't have a shot.*

I pushed harder, breaking into the clearing, and then stopped dead. Fighting was happening in several arenas. Kingston and Locke were in their human forms, Puck was in his wolf's, but I only had eyes for Wren.

A man with dark hair and leering eyes had her by the throat and was dragging her from a fucking cage. A growl tore from my mouth, and I poised to spring, but then Wren pulled something from her waistband and stabbed the man in the heart. He dropped to the ground.

He stared up at nothing as his blood pooled beneath him. A roar of appreciation escaped me, and I bounded toward Wren. Her gaze snapped up at my approach, and I wished I could mind-speak to her now, tell her how proud I was of her. But I wouldn't have that ability until we all were mated to her.

Instead, I settled for headbutting her side and licking her chin. Wren's fingers sank into my fur. "Brix," she whispered.

Relief swept through me. She was okay. Alive. Breathing.

"Get her!" a man hollered, lifting a rifle in my direction.

Kingston leveled an answering weapon at him at the last possible moment and hit the man square between the eyes. He fell, but the two with him shifted and ran straight for us.

King tried to get off another shot but got pulled into a hand-to-hand battle with another man. I let out a low growl, bracing for the two wolves coming straight for Wren and me. Wren took up a fighting stance, her knife at the ready.

One of the wolves leapt into the air, aiming for Wren, but just as his jump reached its apex, an arrow hit him directly in the eye. I didn't have a chance to admire Ender's aim because I was too busy taking on wolf number two. The gold-and-brown wolf lunged, but I raked my claws across its flank as I dodged.

The wolf howled and snarled in response. He turned to face me head-on as my brothers battled the others. Saliva dripped from his fangs, and I couldn't help but wonder if he was drugged up, too.

He lunged again, nipping my already injured shoulder, but I dove to the side and rolled. Up on my paws again, I struck out. The golden wolf howled in pain but kept right on coming. I had no choice.

As he lunged a third time, I caught him by the neck. One swift jerk and I felt his spine crack. The wolf fell limply to the ground. Such a waste. And all because the creature had become indoctrinated by Bastian Boudreaux.

It was as if the shifter had some hold over them, feeding the darkness that lived inside and growing it.

"We have to move now," Kingston shouted as he ran over to us. "Locke's boosting one of their vehicles."

As if to punctuate the point, the sound of an engine sprang

to life in the distance. King pulled Wren into his arms and kissed her head. "You're okay."

She nodded quickly. "Let's move."

Ender sailed in on some kind of rope pulley he'd strung between the trees and dropped to the ground just as Puck ran over, still in his wolf form. Ender instantly had his bow and arrow ready as we moved toward the sound of the incoming vehicle.

Then, a voice boomed from the main house. "Do not let the traitor live!"

Everything happened in slow motion.

A man stepped from the building, a rifle lifted. Ender turned, aiming his arrow. Both shot at the same time. Ender's hit true, striking the man right between the eyes. But the man's bullet also made contact.

Kingston moved, shoving Wren to the side, but he wasn't quick enough. The bullet hit him right in the chest. His eyes widened, flashing to his wolf as pain speared him. His body hit the ground with thundering force, and then the world went quiet.

CHAPTER SIX

Wren

Everything came in sharp, jerky flashes. The sound of the bullet. Kingston shoving me to the side. Him falling to the ground. All the blood.

A massive SUV jerked to a stop just outside the clearing, and some part of me recognized Locke behind the wheel and a back door opening, Hera at the ready.

Ender's arrows flew, raining down on anyone who stepped into view, but I only had eyes for King. Blood had soaked through his tee, spreading too fast and far. Puck shifted, lifting King into his arms and hurrying for the SUV as Ender provided cover. I slid into the rear seat with the rest of them, and Ender and Brix leapt into the back.

"Help him," I croaked at Hera.

Her face paled as she took in Kingston's form. His eyes were closed now, his breathing shallow.

"Please," I begged her.

"Hands on his chest, over the wound. Press as hard as you can," she instructed.

I moved instantly, kneeling on the floorboard and putting all my weight into the contact.

King's eyes fluttered, and he let out a pained groan.

"I'm sorry," I whispered. "I'm so sorry."

His eyes opened, heavy-lidded and trying to focus. "Wren..."

"I'm here. Just hold on. We're going to fix you up. Just hold on."

"Love...you...best honor...of my...life...loving you," he rasped.

Tears streamed down my cheeks, mixing with King's blood in a horrible sort of beauty as they fell. "Don't leave me. Please, don't leave me."

His lashes fluttered again, and this time, his eyes fell closed.

"How close to the safe house?" Hera barked.

"Five minutes out," Locke called.

"Make it three," she ordered. "Did you stock it with my supplies?"

"Of course we did," Puck growled as he pulled on a shirt to go with the sweats he'd obviously pulled from somewhere in the vehicle. Since the SUV belonged to shifters, it wasn't all that surprising to find extra clothes, but I saw his nose wrinkle at the enemy's scent.

Hera pulled a pouch from her pocket and sprinkled the contents over King. "This won't help for long, but it will hold him for now."

She began chanting, and light illuminated the SUV, sparks that circled and danced, hovering over King. My gaze moved between the light, Hera, and Kingston. Her face grew paler by the second, and I somehow knew she didn't have much left in her reserves.

I closed my eyes, lifting prayers to the gods of nature and the universe, begging them not to take King from me when we'd only just begun.

Tires screeched, and we jerked to a stop. The sparks blinked out, and then we were moving again. Puck and Ender lifted King out of the vehicle, carrying him toward a cabin I didn't recognize.

"On the table," Hera yelled, running for the kitchen island.

I stayed right at King's side, gripping his hand as they set him on the hard surface. He groaned, but his eyes never opened. I could feel him slipping away. The tethers not yet binding us were fading.

Hera moved to the table, barking out orders. She cut the shirt from King's body, and fresh blood pooled. She cursed, and her gaze snapped to me. "You're his only hope. You have to keep him here."

"How? Tell me what to do. I'll do it."

"You need to bite him. Bond yourself to him. It may be enough to save him."

The guys instantly started shouting.

"It could kill her!" Puck yelled.

"King would never want to put her at risk like that," Locke argued.

Everything about it was wrong. A one-sided bond would be a disaster in the long run, but I also knew exactly why Hera had suggested it. We could draw strength from our bondmates, and right now, that was what King needed the most.

He'd been willing to give his life for me, and I would do the same for him.

My canines lengthened, pressing through my gums. Before anyone could stop me, I bit Kingston's shoulder, sending all my love, strength, and hope with the bite. Sensations swept through me—pleasure and pain, hope and fear. Wave after wave until I felt a mental click.

I gently pulled my teeth from King's flesh and wiped away the tiny specks of blood. Below the bite, a mark began to appear. A heart half-covered in what looked like hand wraps from the gym. A choked cry left my lips.

"Take his hand," Hera ordered. "Keep him here."

I gripped King's hand as hard as I could. My vision blurred as she went to work with a mix of medical and magical tactics. King's energy started to fade, and I pushed more of mine into him.

I swayed on my feet, and Locke instantly moved in to steady me. "It's too much," he said.

"No," I rasped. "He's not leaving. I won't let him."

"Almost there," Hera called.

Her hand hovered over King's chest, and the bullet sprang free. The moment it did, her hand clamped over the wound, and she began to chant. But it was too much. Everything in me started to waver. The room tipped sideways, and then I couldn't see anything at all.

CHAPTER SEVEN

Wren

I WOKE TO A BURNING HEAT AS IF I WERE LYING ON SAND baked by the sun, the kind that scalded your feet if you stayed put too long. I let out a grumbling groan, and the surface I was lying on shifted. Was some kind of weird earthquake happening?

My eyelids fluttered, and bright light swept through in flashes. I took in everything I could before they closed again. Each sweep gave me more information. A rustic cabin, but one that was that way by choice. I knew because all the furniture looked fancy.

A cloud-like bed with a thick comforter. A bare, muscular chest. An angry scar.

The last image had me jerking upright.

"Easy," Kingston said, the tone of his voice unreadable.

"Oh, gods." I shoved my hair out of my face, struggling to process what I saw. King was propped up against the pillows and had color back in his face. It was no longer a sickly shade of pale. He looked…good. The scruff on his face was thicker, and he somehow looked more muscular, but his eyes… Shadows swirled in the pale-blue, gray swirls streaking across his irises.

"Are you…you're okay?" I croaked.

"I'm fine." A muscle pulsed in Kingston's jaw. "How do you feel? Are you in pain?"

I did a mental sweep. I felt rough, sore muscles and an ache that lived in my bones. Given what I'd been through in the past few days, it made sense. And then I remembered the bite. The bond.

My gaze moved to King's shoulder and the mark there. A heart wrapped in something that signified both our fighting natures, in practice and in our souls. My fingers itched to reach out and touch it, to stroke every line.

"Why?" Kingston rasped. "Why did you do it?"

My eyes flew to his face, and I saw it then—the anger pulsing behind the mask. "What do you mean?"

"You bonded us," he growled. "You could've been killed."

I felt my eyes flash to my wolf. My inner beast wanted to rake her claws across King. "You were *dying*."

"I would've survived," Kingston ground out.

I threw off the covers and pushed out of bed. "Is being mated to me truly that horrible?"

King shoved up and raked a hand through his hair. "I *never* wanted you to mate me because you were forced to."

Anger burned brighter, stoked by frustration and grief. "Did you even consider that maybe I did it because I love you?"

I stomped by him and into the bathroom, slamming the door behind me. Tears burned my eyes, but I refused to let them fall. Kingston already had my soul for all eternity. He didn't deserve my tears, too.

Crossing to the sink, I took in my reflection. The bathroom's dark tones were mirrored in my face: deep purple swaths of color beneath my eyes, an almost gray hue to my skin. What I'd done for King had cost me.

I shoved away from the sink and moved to the shower, turning it on. The water hit the elaborate black marble. It fit the gold fixtures and the hunter-green walls perfectly, but I couldn't find it in me to enjoy it.

Instead, I peeled off the T-shirt someone had put me in and tossed my underwear on top of it. Stepping into the shower, I groaned as the spray hit me. The warmth was a balm.

I leaned my head against the wall and let the water rain down on me. Then, the tears fell. Silent at first, and then in big, racking sobs. I couldn't hold them in. It was too much.

The threats Marcelle had leveled at me. My father's cruelty. Almost losing King. His rejection now.

I was breaking and could do nothing to stop it.

The shower door opened, and I whirled around. King stood there, stripped down to nothing, pure agony in the lines of his face. "Wren," he rasped.

"Don't," I lashed out. "You don't get to sweep in and comfort me now. Not when you don't want this."

He moved in, ignoring my words, and pulled me into his arms. "I want this more than my next breath. There's nothing in this world I want *more* than a life with you. But it killed something in me to think you initiated the bond out of some sense of duty."

I started crying harder, but Kingston held me through every sob. He didn't let go as my body shook against his. He held on until my tears slowed and my breathing settled.

His fingers slid through the wet tangle of my hair, and he tipped my head back. "I love you, Wren. I love you with everything I have and everything I am. I love you. I'm yours. In every way that matters."

I looked up into those pale-blue eyes. There were still shadows there, but there was also hope. "Make me yours," I whispered, my voice raw.

"Wren, you've been through so much."

"Please. It's what I need. You."

Kingston leaned in, his mouth taking mine in a slow kiss. "First, I take care of my little warrior."

My breath hitched as he moved me back into the spray. King gently tipped my head back to wet my hair again. He reached for the shampoo on the shower shelf and squeezed some into his hands. The scent of jasmine filled the shower, and I moaned as Kingston began massaging my scalp.

He took his time, soaping every strand and rinsing every speck away. He followed the pattern again with the conditioner, his fingers pressing against my skull with the most delicious pressure as more of that jasmine scent swirled around us.

King's nose slid down the column of my throat. "Being away from you was like losing a piece of my soul. I tried to pull up every memory, playing them over and over again so I wouldn't lose the feel of you, the scent, the taste."

His tongue flicked out as if to punctuate his point, and heat built low in my belly. Kingston reached for the bodywash, soaping his hands and running them down my arms. As he rinsed it away, he ran his lips over an especially bad scar. "I'd do anything to erase this. Not the mark. That proves your strength. But the pain. I'd do anything to erase the pain."

"King," I croaked.

He sank to his knees, soaping one leg and then the other. "I love you, Wren. Everything about you is a miracle."

Kingston guided the water over one leg and then the other, but he didn't rise. He stayed on his knees, gazing up at me with such reverence. His hand slid up one thigh, higher and higher, until he parted me.

A gasp slipped free, and his fingers teased and toyed. I gripped King's shoulders, trying to hold on. Because having his touch now… it was so much more.

The half-completed bond sang through my nerve endings, crying out to be fulfilled. My flesh ached for King's teeth, for his canines to pierce my skin in a bite that meant forever. I craved it like nothing I'd ever experienced.

Kingston slid two fingers inside me on a slow glide. "So fucking perfect. Just feeling you on my fingers is heaven."

My walls tightened around him at the words, and King groaned. Then, he leaned in closer and inhaled deeply. "Killing me, Little Warrior. But what a way to go."

His tongue flicked out, circling my clit. A wave of pleasure shot through me, but fast on its heels came a craving for more. For everything.

Kingston's fingers swirled inside before sliding out and thrusting in again. He worked me with his fingers and tongue, a shudder racing through me. I had to brace one hand on the wall to stay upright.

"Please," I begged.

King knew what I was asking for, the ultimate piece of him. Of us. His lips left that bundle of nerves and moved to my thigh as his fingers kept moving inside me. His mouth hovered over my flesh, and then he sank his teeth into me.

My orgasm was instantaneous and so intense my knees buckled. But Kingston kept me upright. He sucked on my bond mark as his fingers thrust in and out of me. Wave after wave crashed over me until I had nothing left to give.

As I collapsed, King caught me and cradled me in his arms. "I've got you. And I always will."

CHAPTER EIGHT

Puck

"Do you think I should go in there? I feel like I should go in there," I said as I pushed back from the long table that had served as King's operating room and now had a brunch spread to rival all brunch spreads atop it.

Brix reached out and clamped a hand on my shoulder, keeping me from rising. My gaze flicked to him. I still wasn't used to the casualness with which Brix made human contact.

"They need to work it out," Brix said calmly.

"Wren was yelling," I argued.

Ender took a sip of coffee. "King probably said something moronic."

"You'd know all about that," Locke muttered.

Ender glared in our resident hacker's direction as Hera tried to cover her laugh with a napkin. He turned that glare on her. "Got something to say, witch?"

Hera's pale-green eyes flashed a deeper color, and sparks of energy zapped across the space, landing on Ender.

"Ow! Shit!" Ender jerked, spilling coffee on his shirt. "Seriously?"

"You know that term isn't appreciated." She took a bite of the egg casserole I'd spent hours on as we waited for Wren to wake. "But this is. Thank you, Puck."

"Least I could do." We'd never be able to repay Hera for what she'd done. We'd all seen what it cost her. Not the same as Wren, but enough that she'd gone to one of the bedrooms and slept for thirteen hours straight.

A phone dinged, and Brix pulled it out of his pocket. "Plane's ready whenever we are."

Good. That was good. We needed to get the hell out of Louisiana before Bastian and the Red River pack had a chance to recover. I glanced at Ender. "Any word from your source?"

Ender was protective of his informants, never divulging their identities. But he was beyond secretive about one in particular. We knew nothing about them except that they were plugged into the darkest places in the supernatural world and had an otherworldly knowledge of the happenings there.

Ender flipped his phone over and shook his head. "Not yet. I don't think we should move until we hear from him."

Hera's lips pursed. "We should get out of here as quickly as possible."

"Trust me," Ender gritted out. "We want his insight."

"I don't trust you, so—"

Her voice cut off as footsteps came from the back hallway. Everyone turned at once, and Wren froze, her cheeks heating. "Hi," she squeaked.

She looked fucking adorable with her hair wrapped in a towel and barefoot. She wore tiny shorts and an oversized tee, but my gaze stilled on the fresh mark on her thigh.

A grin split my face as I looked at the man behind her. "The thigh, King? Seriously?"

Wren's blush deepened, and she turned into Kingston. He glared at me and simply lifted her into his arms. "We don't need your brand of bullshit this morning."

"Bullshit?" I demanded with false affront. "I'm just calling 'em like I see 'em."

Hera threw a biscuit at me, and I caught it easily. She looked at the newly mated couple. "How are you both feeling?"

Kingston crossed to the table and lowered himself and Wren to a chair. "I feel great." He lifted Wren's chin, his fingers ghosting over where dark circles had been. "You, Little Warrior?"

She brushed her lips across his. "Perfect."

A low, rumbling growl emanated from his chest, and she laughed, trying to slide off his lap. King's hold on her tightened, a different kind of growl leaving him then. Newly mated pairs could be territorial in the first few hours and days after the bond, but the fact that Kingston was the alpha would heighten those instincts.

"Stay," he rumbled. "Need you close."

Wren ran her nose along the column of his throat, soothing the beast inside him. "Okay. But I need food." Her stomach rumbled in agreement.

I so badly wanted to pull her to me, kiss her, and lose myself in her. I knew we all wanted that after fearing the worst. But if any of us made a move like that right now, King would take our heads off. We had to give him space. So, I did the only thing I could. I piled a plate high with food for Wren.

"Here," I said, sliding it over to her. "Eat every last piece."

Wren's eyes widened. "Uh, buddy? I'm not a linebacker for a professional football team."

Something shifted in my chest at the use of the nickname. I made a face. "Birdie, I am *not* your buddy."

Her lips twitched. "Sure, you aren't."

King sent me a look. "What about me? I don't get food?"

"You're hogging our mate. Get your own damn food."

He barked out a laugh but began dishing up a plate for himself.

Locke toyed with the fork in his hand and glanced at Wren. "You're really okay?"

She swallowed a bite of pancake and reached over to squeeze his hand. "I didn't feel great when I woke up, but after we, um, bonded, I felt amazing. It's like everything healed."

"It's the balance being restored," Hera said. "Everything you gave to Kingston returned to you now that he's healed."

Wren looked up at King, her hand moving to stroke his cheek. "We're okay."

He dropped a kiss to the top of her head. "We're okay."

A phone began ringing, and Ender shoved back from the table, answering it with a gruff, "Speak."

Wren made a face. "Only Ender would answer a phone call like that."

Brix choked on a laugh. "He's got a way."

Still, we all followed him with our eyes as he stepped out onto the cabin's front porch. He paced back and forth as he spoke, grabbing his deep-brown man bun and giving it a tug. The lines of strain around his mouth didn't speak of good things, and the food I'd eaten suddenly felt heavy in my gut.

In seconds, Ender was striding back inside, slamming the door behind him.

"What?" Kingston demanded.

Ender's amber eyes flashed gold. "They're reassembling." His gaze flicked down to Wren for the briefest of moments before returning to King. "Bastian took his beta to a local dark mage coven. They brought him back."

The entire room went silent. I wasn't sure a single person even breathed.

Bringing someone back from the dead carried a price no one had the reserves to pay. It meant a blood sacrifice. And more than that, the person who returned wasn't the same as the one who was lost. They were darker.

Given that Marcelle was already evil incarnate, I didn't even want to think about what he'd return as. But worse? He'd come for the one who'd ended his life.

He'd come for Wren.

CHAPTER NINE

Wren

I'd never been on a plane before. When I was a child, and Mom and I were running, we couldn't risk that sort of travel. And when I was in my teens and early twenties, trying to hide from Bastian, I couldn't exactly afford it. So, having my first flight be on some fancy-pants private jet had my head spinning.

The plane jostled me as it hit some turbulence, and my fingers dug into the seat. Locke reached over and covered my hand with his. "It's okay. It's perfectly normal. We'll be on the ground in twenty minutes."

I nodded in a staccato beat I was sure made me look more than a little unhinged. The truth was, my nerves were ratcheted up to an eleven. The entire three-hour drive to the airstrip, I'd been braced for attack, half-expecting Marcelle to swoop in from the sky and demand my soul.

A shiver raced through me at the thought, and Locke

moved instantly. Unbuckling my seat belt, he lifted me into his lap and nuzzled me in the way he always did when I needed the contact. A little of the tension bled out of me. "Thank you," I whispered.

He traced a hand up and down my back. "We won't let him get to you."

Kingston leaned forward and took my hand. "We'll take every precaution. Heightened security. Nowhere alone. Patrols of Crescent Creek."

I wanted to believe that I would be safe now. But I knew the truth. I wouldn't be. Not until Bastian and Marcelle were wiped from this earth.

"We have to kill them." I swallowed hard as if giving voice to the words had created a wound. "Both of them. There'll be no peace for any of us until then. It's foolish to think otherwise."

Kingston opened his mouth to speak, but Ender cut him off. "She's right. We have to end them both. They'll keep coming for her. There's nothing more important to them now."

I locked my gaze with Ender's amber one. The tension between us crackled in the air, but it was like neither of us knew how to fix it.

Locke's hand moved, his thumb stroking the back of my neck. "We need to be careful. Thoughtful. We can't rush into anything rash."

"We need to bring them to us," Brix said.

Puck frowned and leaned forward. "That happened last time. It didn't work out so well for us."

Brix shook his head. "We thought Bastian would either snatch her when she was unprotected or attack us at home. Now, we know how his mind works. He won't get that element of surprise again."

That much was true. If distraction came, we knew what was at the heart of it. My chest ached. I wanted to see Clyde and make sure he was really okay. I wanted to see Juan and Franco, too. We'd all been through so much. And all because of my hateful father.

"His pack is fractured," I said, anger humming in my vocal cords. "Some are truly loyal, but more are simply terrified. If we give them another option, they may not stand with him."

Kingston's hand gripped mine tighter as a small smile tugged at his lips. "My mate is a mastermind."

A small laugh broke free from my lips. "I'm not sure I'd go that far."

King glanced at Ender. "Do you think you can get word to some strategic people in Red River? Offer them refuge?"

Ender frowned. "We'll have to wait. And it will have to be offered in battle. Otherwise, it gives Bastian an opportunity to send a plant."

King grimaced. "You're right."

I shivered against Locke. "The women on the compound... Some truly want to be there and revel in Bastian's evil. But so many more want to be free. And Bastian...he's taken everything from them. Even their shoes."

"Their shoes?" Puck asked.

I nodded, pain slicing across my sternum. "So they can't run. Marcelle said it was punishment for what I'd done."

The guys all cursed.

King squeezed my hand. "We'll get them out. I promise."

"I'm sorry, sir. Ma'am," the dapperly dressed flight attendant said before gesturing to the seat belt light. "We'll be landing soon. Please buckle your belts."

Locke let out a rumbling growl that made me laugh. I kissed him quickly. "I'll sit with you on the car ride."

"What about me?" Puck pouted.

"You, too, buddy."

He scowled. "Birdie..."

I only grinned wider.

Ender slowed the SUV to a stop in front of our house. I'd never been so happy to see a structure in my life. I could've kissed the ground as we all slid out.

Inhaling deeply, I took in the scents of the pine trees around us, the creek water in the distance, and the last of the wildflowers blooming.

A ding sounded, and Ender pulled out his phone, scowling at the screen.

"What is it?" Brix asked.

"Just my source," he muttered.

I frowned at Ender. "Who is this source, anyway?"

Ender's spine snapped straight. "That's none of your concern."

I bristled at his tone, but, more than that, the slap of his words hurt. It was a clear "*back off.*" And even though I was used to that from Ender, it didn't soften the sting. "It *is* my concern if your source is the one who told Bastian where I was in the first place. Did you ever consider that?"

Ender's breaths came quicker. "He would never betray me like that."

I let out a huff of breath. "At least I know it's a *he* now. But that's all we know, and we deserve a hell of a lot more."

Ender's jaw worked back and forth. "You should trust my judgment."

I laughed, but there was no warmth in the tone. "*Trust*? There's nothing but secrets with you. There's nothing *to* trust."

Ender's eyes flashed gold, and then he turned and stalked away. Just like always.

My shoulders slumped, and pressure built behind my eyes.

"It's not you," Brix said quietly. "It's just not how he's built."

I shook my head. "He's right about one thing. You can't build a relationship without trust. But you can't just demand it without giving any in return."

And I wasn't sure Ender would ever be capable of giving that.

CHAPTER TEN

Ender

I stalked through the forest, the small animals scampering to get out of my way. *Good.* They should run.

Gods, I was an ass. In every way someone could be.

Picking up a rock, I threw it as hard as I could at a tree. Bark flew, and a wound remained. Even though Kingston had been the one injured, *I* felt like the damn tree. As if my chest had a hole that would never be filled.

A twig snapped behind me, and I braced. Whoever it was wasn't trying to disguise their footsteps. That was smart. They could've ended up with an arrow in the shoulder if they had.

The wind shifted, and Brix's scent caught on the breeze. Of course, it was him. It felt like a low blow, the pack sending the one person they knew I wouldn't ream out because we'd shared too much.

Brix came to stand beside me, staring out at the creek and

the forest beyond. He was quiet for a long while. "It's Rhys, isn't it? Your source?"

My back teeth ground together. "Yes."

Brix was the only one who'd ever met the man. Rhys and I had traded more life debts than I cared to remember. But it was more. I knew what it was like to need to escape a past existence and start over.

"I won't be responsible for ruining Rhys's chances at a new life by exposing him. Not even to Wren."

Brix turned to face me, studying me for a long moment, those wheels clearly turning. "Are you sure this is about protecting Rhys and not about pushing Wren away?"

Annoyance flared. "Of course, it's about protecting Rhys."

"So, you're telling me you're not scared shitless by how much you care about Wren?"

I bristled. "She's my mate. Of course, I care about her."

One corner of Brix's mouth kicked up. "Good to hear you call her your mate."

"Fuck off." Just saying the word made me feel twitchy. My wolf pushed at my skin, wanting out, wanting to be free. I hadn't let him run in far too long. I was too afraid he'd hunt Wren down and bite her. He thought I was a fool.

And he was right. But I couldn't see a path through. Couldn't figure out how to fix all the ways I'd fucked up. So, I just kept digging the hole deeper.

"You know you don't have to reveal *what* Rhys is to tell Wren *who* he is. She just wants to know if she can trust this anonymous stranger. Wouldn't you want the same?" Brix pressed.

A snarl left my lips. "Why do you have to make a perfectly good point?"

Brix slapped me on the shoulder and gave me a little shake. "You're welcome." He held on for a moment. "Don't fuck this up, End."

His words hit something deep in my chest, causing it to rattle around in the hollowness there. But it was more. "You're touching me."

I couldn't remember the last time Brix and I'd had any contact that wasn't sparring or related to ink. But here he was, his hand on my shoulder, not letting go.

Brix's lips twitched. "Don't make it weird." Then he released me and headed back toward the house. To Wren. Because she was the one who'd grounded him, *healed* him.

The feeling of that echoing hollowness intensified, and I felt more alone than I ever had. And it was my fault. I knew I didn't want my life to look like this. I just couldn't seem to figure out how to make it any different, how to heal what I'd broken. Because right now, those fractures and fissures felt irrevocable.

My phone rang, cutting through my downward spiral of self-pity. I pulled it out and glowered at the screen. "What?"

"Is that any way to greet your bestest friend?" Rhys's raspy amusement filled the line, only intensifying my glare.

"Brix is my best friend."

"Ouch. That hurts. Thrown over for the broody one."

It wasn't as if Rhys didn't have broodiness in spades at times. He just liked to cover it with his mercurial nature.

"Did you find something else?" I asked.

Rhys was quiet for a moment. "Something's wrong. You're more cantankerous than usual."

"Protecting your ass is getting me in deep shit."

A different sort of energy crackled across the line. "Someone's asking about me? Who?"

The undertone to Rhys's words made it clear that he'd be ending whoever was doing it.

"Not like that," I ground out. "Stow your sharp implements."

"Then who?" Rhys growled, not amused.

"Wren." It was the honest truth, a single word, but it felt unbelievably difficult to say.

There was silence for a moment, and then Rhys burst out laughing.

"It's not fucking funny," I snarled.

"I beg to disagree. That mate of yours is giving you a run for your money."

It was a hell of a lot more than that, but I didn't want to go there. "You could show a little understanding. It's your fault I'm in hot water."

"How in the world is that possible?" Rhys asked.

"She wants to know who my source is."

"And you didn't tell her?" This time, Rhys sounded aghast.

My back teeth ground together. "Wasn't it you who threatened to remove my head from my body if I told anyone your secrets?"

Rhys sighed. "You don't have to reveal my secrets to tell Wren who I am. She's your mate, for fuck's sake. It has to be painful for her to have you hiding this sort of thing from her."

My hand fisted, claws lengthening until they pricked my palm. "You sound like Brix."

"At least one of you has some sense."

"Fuck off."

"Sorry, far too invested now. I think I need to meet this mate of yours."

Tension bled into my muscles. "Don't even think about it."

"What's the matter, End? Afraid she'll leave your cranky ass behind?"

I was already terrified of that. Because the truth was, if I were Wren, I wouldn't want a damn thing to do with me.

CHAPTER ELEVEN

Wren

I WOKE TO SUNLIGHT STREAMING THROUGH THE WINDOWS, illuminating the pack bedroom. As I stretched in the empty bed, a soft meow sounded. "Princess," I cooed.

She moved in, butting her head against the underside of my chin. I cuddled her against me. "I missed you so much."

She started to purr like a locomotive, and I couldn't help but grin. As my gaze moved to the couch on the far wall, the grin slipped a fraction. A blanket that hadn't been there before was folded over the arm.

Ender.

He'd avoided me for the rest of yesterday, going the gods only knew where. My stomach twisted at the thought. I did *not* want to go there.

"Why is he like this?" I muttered to Princess.

She let out a chattering meow in answer. I took it as her agreement.

Glancing at the clock, I winced. Half past ten? I never slept this late. And the fact that I was in bed alone said the guys had already started their days. Apparently, I still needed to catch up on rest even though my body had healed.

"We gotta get up, baby."

Princess bit my chin in response.

A laugh bubbled out of me. "You certainly make your wishes known, don't you? Don't worry, you can come with me."

She let out a warbling meow, and I threw back the covers, making my way to the bathroom. I pulled out the stool to the vanity so Princess could sit with me and made quick work of getting ready and changing into workout clothes. I needed to move my body and ease back into training. Most of all, I needed to see Clyde.

"Ready?" I asked Princess.

She let out a meow and leapt from the stool onto my shoulder. I lifted a hand and scratched under her chin. "That's my girl."

We made our way downstairs and in the direction of the voices below. As I got closer, I picked out four of the five guys. I wasn't sure if it was relief or annoyance that swept through me at the absence of Ender's deep tenor. But when I stepped into the kitchen, I found him among the fray.

I came up short as his amber eyes lifted and settled on the cat on my shoulder.

"How come she loves you so much? She hates me," Puck pouted.

"She senses your evil," Ender muttered, sipping his coffee.

King moved into my space, kissing my temple and giving Princess a scratch. "How are you feeling? You were sleeping so soundly we didn't want to wake you."

"I feel good," I said, leaning into him and soaking up his strength, warmth, and comfort. "I think I needed those extra hours."

"You need extra calories, too," Puck said, sliding a plate in my direction.

It was heaped high with eggs, fruit, and what looked like some sort of elaborate French toast. My stomach rumbled. "What is that?" I asked, pointing to the confection on the plate.

"Frosted Flakes French toast," Locke mumbled around a bite. "It's so freaking good."

My lips twitched. "Sounds like it."

Locke just grinned and kept chewing. "Can't stop, won't stop."

Princess leapt from my shoulder and meandered around the stools at the island to see if anyone would give her food. I slid onto an empty seat, and Brix leaned over to give me a quick kiss. "Missed you."

I smiled against his mouth. "It's only been a couple of hours."

"Still missed you."

"Me, too," I whispered.

A stool scraped against the tile floor, and my head jerked up to see Ender stalking toward the coffee pot. I stuck out my tongue at his back, and Puck burst out laughing.

"Fuck. I missed you, too, Birdie."

"I do like to keep things interesting," I said, cutting into a piece of my French toast. I took a bite, and my eyes instantly closed as I let out a moan. "This is the best thing I have ever tasted in my entire life."

When I opened my eyes, it was to find five other sets locked on my mouth. I flushed. "Sorry."

Puck leaned across the island and licked a stray drop of syrup from my bottom lip. "Never apologize for enjoying what I make you."

"Told you it was the bomb," Locke said, cutting another bite.

Kingston's mouth quirked. "Okay, nineties child."

Locke flipped him off.

"So," Puck said, leaning back against the counter, "what do you want to do today?"

"I need to go to Crescent Kingdom," I said instantly.

King stiffened. "I was thinking we could stay on territory for a while. Until we know what's what."

I shook my head. "I need to see Clyde, and I wouldn't mind a light workout to loosen up my muscles."

Little worry lines took root in Locke's brow. "Are you sure you're ready for that? You've been through a lot."

"I won't push it. But I need to get moving again. I need to be ready."

The room went quiet at that. Because they knew exactly what I needed to be ready for.

A muscle in Ender's jaw pulsed in a staccato beat. "We all go, then. You're never alone."

Great, just great. The king of the brood would be my constant shadow. Perfect.

CHAPTER TWELVE

Wren

I felt like the President of the United States. Or maybe the Queen of England. The guys surrounded me like bodyguards, their heads on a swivel as we walked from the SUV to the gym. Since I'd arrived in Colorado, Crescent Kingdom had been my safe space, but it lost a little of its sheen when it seemed like the guys could pull a weapon at any moment.

I tried not to let my annoyance flare. I knew they were doing it out of protection and care, but I couldn't help feeling stifled. I closed my eyes briefly, breathing in the pine air and remembering that I was free, even if it didn't feel that way at the moment.

Fingers slid through mine, and my eyes opened to find Brix at my side. "It won't be forever," he whispered. "I promise."

Something about the simple touch, reassurance, and understanding soothed my raw edges. "Thank you." I leaned into him, soaking up the connection as our bond hummed.

Ender strode forward and into the gym. I began to follow, but Kingston held up a hand. "Wait. Just a moment."

My fingers tightened around Brix's because I knew why King was having me wait. Ender was sweeping the building. An extra measure of security.

A few moments later, Ender reemerged. "We're good."

The air left my lungs with a whoosh. The idea of Bastian making my friends at the gym a target *again* reminded me just how much was at stake. A hell of a lot more than just me was at risk.

As we moved into the gym, all eyes came to us. Clyde froze, his eyes getting glassy as they locked on me. A second later, he was striding across the room in that lumbering gait. Before I could get a word out, he'd hauled me into his arms. "Girlie," he choked out.

"Hey, Gramps," I rasped.

"You're okay? You're really okay?"

I knew King had called him to tell him they had me and that we were on our way home, but it obviously wasn't enough for Clyde. I understood that because I felt the same way about him.

"I'm fine. What about you?" I asked, pulling myself out of his hold and doing a sweep.

"You know no fire's gonna take me out." But the rattling cough he let out said he was still experiencing some aftereffects.

"Wren, girl, you are a sight for sore eyes," Juan said, making his way over. He had a slight limp from the beam that had landed on him, but he looked mostly okay.

And Franco was right behind him, looking healthy and whole. "Damn good to see you," he said.

"You guys, too," I answered, suddenly feeling awkward with all that lay between us.

Clyde's jaw hardened. "Everyone out," he barked. "Emergency gym meeting."

The two guys sparring looked at Clyde as if he were a bit unhinged, and the woman working a heavy bag appeared more than a little annoyed.

"I'll stay open an hour later to make up for it," he called.

"Clyde," Kingston began, his voice low.

"Don't you start with me, boy. We have a conversation that needs having. It's been a long time coming."

A tingling sensation lit across my skin as my nerves ramped up. I sent Brix a slightly panicked look as he took in Clyde, assessing.

We waited silently while the three other patrons got their gear and headed for the parking lot. Clyde followed as they exited, locking the gym door behind them and then turning to face us. "What the hell were those things in the fire because they sure as hell weren't human?"

Panic raced through me as I tried to come up with a plausible excuse. What had Bastian done when he grabbed Clyde? How had he exposed himself? Us?

It went against the supernatural code to reveal our alternate forms or gifts. And it could get you in serious trouble.

"We've known forever," Franco said, crossing his arms. "Too many things don't add up."

Juan grinned. "I still think it's radioactive spider bites."

"Could be aliens," Franco argued. "That makes the most sense statistically."

Kingston scrubbed a hand over his face. "You're right."

"You're fucking aliens?" Juan shrieked.

"Don't," I whispered to King. It was too great a risk. If any of them talked, it could put us on Incantare's radar. Incantare was the law enforcement body of the supernatural world and not an organization you wanted to be in opposition with.

"They already know more than they should," Kingston said. "It's not fair."

"Incantare," Ender growled, voicing my fears.

"We're bound by those laws, but we're also bound by the laws of family," King argued.

He made a damn good point there.

His gaze swept the room, landing on Franco, then Juan, and

finally Clyde. "If you reveal this to a single soul, you'll be putting our lives at risk."

"We ain't snitches, and we ain't traitors," Clyde rumbled. "You saved all our lives. We *owe* you. But more than that. We love you. So, tell us what's going on."

Kingston sighed. "We're shifters. Wolf shifters."

The three humans stared at him.

"I'm sorry...what?" Franco asked.

"Half our nature is human, half is wolf," Kingston explained.

Juan gaped at him. "You're werewolves?"

Growls lit the air, and I couldn't help but smile. "Don't use that term."

His brow furrowed. "Why not?"

Locke began listing off points on his fingers. "We're not forced to change on a full moon. Our bites don't turn someone."

"They do kill, though," Ender warned.

"There's no way," Franco protested.

Puck toed off his shoes and then began pulling off his shirt.

"Dude," Juan muttered. "You're ripped, but I don't swing that way. A striptease isn't going to distract me."

But I knew exactly what he was doing. Puck slid off his joggers so he wore only his boxer briefs.

Juan started backing away. "Okay, this is a little too weird, even for me."

Suddenly, Puck's form began to vibrate. The sound of bones cracking filled the air. And then the human Puck was gone, replaced by a stunning golden wolf with piercing green eyes.

Juan's face went stark white. "Holy fuck."

CHAPTER THIRTEEN

Kingston

I DIDN'T WATCH PUCK. I'D SEEN HIM SHIFT COUNTLESS TIMES. Instead, I watched the humans' reactions. I needed to know if any were showing signs of bolting. Of running for the hills or trying to expose us.

Franco's arms slowly lowered from their crossed position as he gaped at the golden wolf in his presence. Clyde stood with wide, unblinking eyes as his breaths started to come quicker. And Juan, the goddamned idiot, started whistling at Puck. "No way! Come here, boy. Do you like treats? Can I pet you?"

"Uh, Juan? I wouldn't do that if I were you," Brix warned.

Juan didn't listen; he just kept right on calling Puck in that idiotic way. Puck's wolf half wasn't exactly pleased. He lunged, leaping into the air and snapping at Juan's face.

Juan stumbled and fell back onto one of the fight mats. Puck jumped on top of him, his paws on his chest, and snapped again, then growled a low warning.

"Uhhhhh...nice doggy?" Juan asked, seeming about to piss himself.

Wren moved then, swatting Puck's hind end. "Stop it. You're scaring him."

Puck let out a chuff and then a growly, whiny bark as if explaining himself.

"I know he was disrespectful, but he's a loveable idiot, so cut him some slack," she shot back.

Puck pushed off Juan and moved to Wren. He licked her cheek and then settled his head on her shoulder. Wren's hand sifted into his fur, giving him a rubdown for leaving Juan alone.

"I'll be damned," Clyde muttered.

Juan slowly sat up, looking annoyed. "See, he does like dog things. He's getting scratches."

Ender rolled his eyes. "From his *mate*. It's a little different."

"Mate?" Franco asked.

"Our kind has destined mates," I explained. "Females are rare in our species, so they have multiple mates orchestrated by the gods."

"Whoa," Juan exclaimed, climbing to his feet. "That's a whole new meaning to ball and chain."

"Someone hit him," Ender muttered.

"Gladly," Franco said, slapping Juan upside the head.

Juan scowled. "That hurt."

"I meant for it to."

I turned to Clyde, trying to read the expression on my friend's face. "I'm sorry I didn't tell you sooner. There are laws and—"

Clyde waved me off. "I get it. It's a hell of a secret." He looked around at each of us. "So, you all turn into wolves?" His gaze held on Wren. "Even you?"

"Even me," she echoed.

Clyde's eyes narrowed. "But there's something else with you. That man. He would've done anything to get you."

Puck let out a low, rumbling growl at the reminder, and Wren held him tighter to her—whether for her or him, I wasn't sure. She swallowed hard. "He's my father."

"What the fuck?" Franco rasped.

"He's not a good man. There's evil in him," Wren said. "He can't stand that I escaped him, and he'll do anything to bring me down—bring all of us down."

Clyde's gaze cut to me. "What the hell are you doing about that, boy?"

The instant loyalty to Wren eased something in me. It was clear as day that Clyde would do anything to protect her, which meant he wouldn't expose us. "We have to kill him."

"Is he a wolf, too?" Franco asked.

"Yes," Wren answered. "My father is a wolf. And my mother… she was a caster."

Clyde's brow furrowed. "A caster?"

Wren nodded. "You'd likely think of them as witches, but they derive their power from nature itself." She lifted a hand and closed her eyes. The water fountain in the corner flared to life, the liquid turning into pure blue energy as she wielded it.

I'd only felt Wren's caster magic flare a handful of times and had never seen her use her gift quite like this. It was a thing to behold. Beauty and power in equal measure.

"Holy shitballs," Juan said in awe.

Wren grinned, manipulating the power so it swirled around him. "Want to fly?"

He nodded like some feral bobblehead doll.

A second later, the blue energy lifted Juan, floating him around the room in a circle.

"Dude, look at me," Juan called to Franco. "I'm so badass."

"You mean Wren's badass?" Franco corrected drolly.

Wren slowly lowered him to the floor, and Juan stumbled as he caught his footing. An instant later, the water and energy disappeared altogether.

"What can we do to help?" Clyde asked. "How do we get rid of the asshole trying to hurt Wren?"

"Yeah," Juan echoed. "We'll stand with you. I don't care if they can all go hairy beast. I'll take 'em."

Anxiety swept through me as I began shaking my head. "You have no idea what you'd be up against, what all is out there. You have to be incredibly careful. If something feels off, get the hell out. Because they'll be coming here, I have no doubt."

Franco crossed his arms again. "We might not be able to stand against them in hand-to-hand, but we can help in other ways. I'm a hell of a shot. And we can be lookouts."

Locke glanced at me. "We could have one or two of them on the monitors when the time comes."

"If we can bait them into striking while on our territory," Ender argued.

The bickering began in earnest about what—if any—role the humans should play. But I knew we wouldn't be able to keep them out. They cared for Wren too deeply.

"Wait," Juan cut in. "You said we don't know what else is out there. Are there mermaids? Because I got a real thing for Ariel."

I pinched the bridge of my nose. "Someone just shoot me now."

CHAPTER FOURTEEN

Locke

AN EDGINESS HAD SETTLED OVER US AS WE HEADED BACK out into the sunshine. It didn't matter that our conversation with the humans had ended in jokes, or that it was clear they had our backs, their knowing about us was a risk, and we knew it.

Everyone dealt with the edginess in different ways. Brix and Ender had done an especially brutal round of sparring. Puck made endless jokes about Juan trying to pet him. King spent a good hour running through precautionary measures for the gym with Clyde. And Wren…she'd gone quiet.

She'd spent the past hour alternating between running on the treadmill, jumping rope, and hitting the heavy bag, and refused any offers to spar or for someone to hold mitts for her. Every second that passed had her turning more inward.

I didn't have Wren's empathic gifts, but the fact that my wolf was submissive meant that I felt others' emotions more intensely than most. And I could feel the anxiety wafting off Wren in waves.

Ender climbed behind the wheel of the SUV as the rest of us took other seats. Puck and Brix sat in the back, and King took the front passenger seat. The moment I climbed into the middle row after Wren, I tugged her gently onto my lap.

"Locke," she protested.

"Let me have this," I whispered.

Wren pulled back for a moment and studied me. She seemed to find…something because the tension radiating through her muscles eased a fraction, and she curled around me.

My wolf let out a rumbling, contented sound. He'd missed her. So damn much. I had, too. And it scared the hell out of me that we'd almost lost her. My hand shifted under Wren's ponytail, kneading the back of her neck and letting her scent soothe my wolf.

"I picked the wrong damn seat," Puck muttered.

Wren's mouth curved against the skin of my neck. "I'll cuddle with you later, buddy."

"Damn straight, you will," Puck huffed. "And there'll be nothing buddy-like about it."

Brix chuckled.

"Don't you think we should be focusing on things other than getting laid?" Ender ground out.

Puck rolled his eyes. "You're just saying that because you're not getting laid."

Ender's fingers tightened on the wheel as he turned onto the main road out of town. "I'm saying that because I'm partial to breathing. King just brought three humans into this mess. We could get the attention of Incantare, and we're already in the sights of a psycho wolf with a revenge complex."

The bit of tension that had slid out of Wren came back with a vengeance. Her fingers curled into my tee, stretching the cotton as if doing so could ward off her fears.

"Do you have a problem with my leadership?" Kingston growled low.

Ender's gaze flicked to King momentarily before returning to the road. "You know I don't. I just think we need to be prepared for what's coming our way. We need to be mindful."

"We're doing that," Brix said, his voice calm. "But you need to be honest about where this is really coming from. And that's your wolf riding you because you haven't bonded with Wren."

He just had to drop that little bomb when we were all in an enclosed vehicle. We all knew Ender's determination to keep his distance would affect him. His wolf didn't understand his human hang-ups. All his wolf knew was that they'd found their mate, and he wanted to claim her. Now. The fact that his human side was getting in the way would put the two halves at odds.

And it was never good when the wolf and human sides were in opposition.

Ender let out a low growl, shooting off that he was the only one taking the threats against us seriously, and things devolved from there. As the arguing intensified, Wren curled into a tighter ball. She released her hold on me and covered her ears.

I felt it then. The pain this was causing her.

"Make it stop," she croaked.

"Enough!" I barked.

The entire vehicle quieted as Ender slowed to a stop in front of the house.

"You know heightened emotions get to her. Grow the fuck up and deal with your shit." I sent the last of those statements directly to Ender. None of us was perfect, I sure as hell wasn't, but End was the one throwing us off so intensely. And it pissed me the hell off.

Shoving the door open, I cradled Wren against me and stalked toward the house. I balanced her in one arm and punched in the code with the other. Taking the stairs two at a time, I headed for my bedroom. We hardly ever spent time in there, mainly because I spent more of my day in the lair than anywhere else, but right now, Wren needed quiet.

Light filtered into the space through the half-covered windows. The dark blues and grays of the furniture and finishes were meant to bring peace, and I hoped they did that for Wren. I gently laid her on my bed, and she curled up on her side.

"Sorry," she slurred.

"You don't have to be sorry about anything." I brushed some hair that had escaped her ponytail back from her face and took in the lines of strain there. "Headache?"

"Yes." The word was a whisper, as if even speaking it aloud hurt.

I moved quickly then, shutting the curtains so we were in full darkness and then moving to the small fridge in the corner. I pulled out a bottle of water and reached for the jar of herbs on top of the refrigerator. I measured two spoonfuls into the bottle and shook it.

I was back at the bedside in a flash, coaxing Wren into a seated position. "Drink this. It'll help."

Wren's hand moved to her stomach. "I'm not sure I can keep it down."

"You can," I promised. "There's something in it that will help with the nausea." I'd been down the migraine road too many times to count. Mine just usually came from staring at a screen for too long.

Wren's brow furrowed, but she took a testing sip, then another, and then finally downed the whole thing. Within seconds, the lines of strain on her face were fading, and she slid back onto the pillows. "Stay with me?"

I got into bed next to her, but doing so hurt. A stabbing pain lit in my chest because I loved her so damn much, and I was *so* scared of losing her. My hands fisted at my sides as I fought back the other things I was feeling, the ugly stew I didn't want to admit to.

Wren turned onto her side to face me. A different sort of line filled her face, a searching kind. "You keep holding yourself back from me." Her voice was quieter now, fatigue trying to pull her under.

"Sleep," I whispered.

"Why?" Wren pressed, desperation bleeding into her voice.

"We'll talk when you wake," I promised.

She grabbed my tee, fisting the material. "Why?"

I stared back at her, unable to allow her to think the worst. "I'm mad at you," I confessed.

"Mad at me?" she parroted.

I nodded. "I'm furious that you sacrificed yourself for Clyde. I'm terrified that you'll do something like that again and that I'll lose you forever. And I can't live without you, Wren."

"Locke," she whispered.

I pulled her into me, urging her head to my chest. I held tightly, knowing she was safe if she was in my arms. "Sleep. We'll deal with it when you wake."

She tried to argue, but the pull of sleep was too strong. She slipped off, and I kept holding on. Because it was the only thing I could do.

CHAPTER FIFTEEN

Wren

I WOKE SLOWLY, NOT BECAUSE ANYTHING FROM THE OUTSIDE world woke me, but because my wolf was clawing at me. She kept nudging me until my eyes finally fluttered open. In sleep, I'd wound myself around Locke as if forming us into a human chain, refusing to let him go.

I winced and slowly released my vise-like grip. "I'm sorry," I mumbled.

Locke let out a low chuckle. "I'm never going to be mad about being close to you." But I detected a hint of sadness in his words. One I'd do anything to wash away.

I leaned back on the pillows, really taking Locke in. The room was still dark, but I let my shifter side take over so I could make out every detail. He'd removed his glasses at some point, setting them on the bedside table. A piece of his deep-brown hair had fallen across his forehead in the kind of disarray I usually only saw when he was at his computer. And there were circles beneath those beautiful, gray eyes.

Reaching out, my fingers ghosted beneath his eyes as though the featherlight touches could erase the shadows there. "I'm sorry I hurt you."

Locke's eyes turned guarded. "You didn't—"

"I did."

He was quiet for a moment before speaking again. "It scares me. . .how much I love you."

"Me, too," I admitted. The depths in which I cared for every single one of these men—even asshole Ender—scared the hell out of me. I couldn't imagine the shell I would be if I lost any of them.

Locke stared back at me, his gaze sweeping over me like the brush of fingertips. "And I'm mad."

"Okay." I had to take that because I wanted him to tell me how he truly felt and not lock it away.

"What you did was reckless. You could've been killed." The words sounded animalistic, guttural and primal, roaring from somewhere deep inside.

"I couldn't let Bastian hurt Clyde because of me. He's an innocent. I never would've been able to live with myself."

"I know," Locke growled, pulling me so I straddled him, his hands sinking into my hair. "And I love you because you care so deeply for others. Yet part of me wants to lock you away just to keep you from playing the shield."

I understood the urge. How many times had I been furious because one of the guys had taken a risk to protect me? Or the lengths they'd gone to in order to keep me safe? I dropped my head to Locke's, pressing my forehead to his and breathing him in. "Maybe we need to trust each other a little more. Trust that this love we're building will see us through, even if it's terrifying in the moment."

Locke's mouth brushed mine. "I love you."

"I love you, too." I whispered the words over his lips, praying it would be strong enough to carry us beyond whatever was to come.

"I don't want you to be anyone but who you are. I'm sorry I pulled back."

My fingers sifted into his hair, keeping our connection as I straightened so I could really see him. "I get it. Self-protection. And we're talking it through now. I just…I missed you."

Locke's expression softened. "I missed you, too. More than you'll ever know." He raised a hand to cup my face, his thumb tracing my lower lip. "Will you do something for me?"

I cocked my head to one side. "If it's lock myself in some underground bunker until all this is over, the answer is no."

Locke barked out a laugh. "No underground bunkers. I promise."

"Then, yes. I'll do something for you. *Anything* for you."

That soft look was back on Locke's face, the one I loved more than any other expression he wore. He reached over, put on his glasses, and opened the bedside table drawer. He fished out a wooden box and handed it to me.

The box itself was stunning, artwork etched into its surface like a tattoo. Moons and hearts formed a stunning pattern across the lid and down the sides. "It's gorgeous."

"Open it," Locke pressed.

My fingers stilled on the lid for a moment before I lifted it. As I did, my lips parted. Inside was a necklace. A delicate gold chain with a lock pendant. As my fingertips ghosted over the metal, I gasped. "It's enchanted."

A buzz lit in my hand like a stroke to the senses. It was magic meant for me.

"Only you or one of your bondmates can remove it. It's spelled with a locator enchantment. And there's a tracker chip in the lock itself. We'll be able to find you wherever you are."

Tears pressed against the backs of my eyes. "This kind of magic…it isn't easy to come by." And I knew it had a high cost.

Locke's thumb ghosted over my lower lip again. "Worth it. Over and over again."

"It's beautiful," I whispered.

Locke lifted the jewelry and fastened it around my neck. "A reminder of us. That I'm with you always."

I leaned down and brushed my lips over his. "Love you."

"Love you, too."

And then my stomach rumbled.

Locke laughed, lifting me as he stood and slid his feet into his shoes. "Let's get you fed."

"I had other plans," I grumbled.

Locke tapped my ass as he set me down. "Later. Gotta take care of my girl first."

I mumbled something about sex winning out over food but still headed for the door.

We made our way downstairs and toward the sound of voices in the kitchen. I could smell the scents of homemade pasta sauce simmering, and my stomach rumbled again.

"Told you that you needed to eat," Locke said with a grin.

"Yeah, yeah."

Just as we hit the bottom floor, the front door opened. I came up short at the appearance of Ender. His gaze instantly cut to me, and his expression shuttered.

That tiny movement cut deeper than I wanted to admit—the fact that Ender didn't want me to know anything he was thinking or feeling, that he couldn't share even one tiny truth with me.

"Feeling better?" he rasped.

I simply stared at him. Why did he get to ask questions when I couldn't ask any in return?

Ender's cheek started to twitch. "Yes?" he pressed.

"Not sure you have a right to that answer," I told him honestly.

The fluttering in his cheek intensified. "Don't be immature."

I bristled. "How are you feeling, Ender? You seemed stressed in the car. Tense. What's going on?"

He stiffened, his amber eyes burning gold. "What is this? I'm rubber and you're glue?"

"It's making a point," I snapped. "You expect me to jump when you say jump. Answer when you ask. But you won't give me any of that respect back. So, who is truly immature?"

"She has a point," Puck yelled from the kitchen.

"Stop eavesdropping," Ender barked. He cast an annoyed look toward me. "I just wondered if your headache was better. But if you want to play games, fine."

I bit the inside of my cheek to keep from saying something I *really* regretted. "What I want is for you to remove the stick from your ass, get over your shit, and deal with the fact that you might actually—heaven forbid—like me."

Ender's teeth gnashed. "I do not like you."

I scoffed. "What are you? In kindergarten?"

"I don't," he huffed.

But the twitch of his fingers and how his eyes shifted to the side told me differently. I grinned at him. "You are such a liar. But have fun in denial land."

A deep chuckle sounded from the back hall, one I didn't recognize, and then a voice just as deep as the tenor of the laugh spoke. "So, this is the little vixen who has turned your life upside down, End?"

The house erupted at the new voice.

CHAPTER SIXTEEN

Ender

ANGRY SHIFTERS FLEW INTO THE ENTRYWAY, CREATING A wall in front of Wren as the man stepped into the light. I didn't move because I knew the asshole currently making himself known.

Rhys looked part biker, part billionaire, and as much as he was concerned about staying under the radar, those two facts—plus his towering, six-foot-five stature—didn't help with the endeavor. His sharp jaw was currently covered with thick scruff that offset the mirth in his golden-amber eyes. A mirth that was amplified as Kingston leveled a gun at his head.

"Who the hell are you?" King growled.

"And how the hell did you get onto our territory without tripping one of my alarms?" Locke snarled.

I wasn't sure I'd ever seen Locke quite so angry, other than when Wren was in danger. The fact that someone could sneak past his defenses was a threat to everything Locke prized.

Rhys just grinned wider. "I'm Rhys. That asshole's bestie." He pointed at me.

"I told you, Brix is my best friend," I clipped. "What are you doing here?"

King looked back and forth between us, the tension in him easing a bit when he saw I hadn't reached for a weapon, but he still didn't lower his gun.

Rhys's gaze cut to Wren, moving so he could get a better look at her. "Told you. I wanted to meet the girl that turned your world upside down."

I bared my teeth at him. "So, you broke onto our pack lands to do it? Haven't you heard of ringing the damn bell?"

Rhys simply shrugged. "What's the fun in that?"

"I want to know how you got past my system," Locke ground out.

I sighed and cracked my neck. "Trust me when I say, it's not your system's fault."

Locke looked between us. "Explain."

"A vampire." The voice was new, feminine, and more than a little curious. Hera moved in from the house's living room and library wing, where she'd clearly been napping given the state of her hair.

As she spoke the words, a new set of growls lit the air. But Wren's wasn't one of them. Instead, she glanced at me, shock evident in her turquoise eyes. "You're friends with a vampire?"

I understood the surprise. Shifters and vampires weren't typically on the same side of things. Maybe because a wolf bite could kill a vampire, and a vampire could turn a wolf into a kind of half-crazed demon. But there were exceptions to every rule.

"Don't worry, Little Vixen," Rhys told Wren. "I don't bite." His ring-ladened fingers lifted to his mouth. "Oh, wait…"

Puck's lip curled as he let out a low growl. "Back up."

I moved in then, not wanting things to devolve. "Relax. Rhys is a dick, but he's not going to harm anyone in this house. Right, Rhys?"

Rhys drummed his fingers over his lips. "That all depends. If someone makes a move on me, I will retaliate."

"But no one will do that if you just behave," I ground out.

Hera moved in closer, her head cocking to one side in a very shifter-like movement. "You're a vampire, but there's something else there, too."

If I didn't know Rhys so damn well, I would've missed it. The slight flicker in his eyes and the way the gold burned a little brighter. He quickly covered it with his impression of a charming smile. "If you're saying I'm special…of course, I am."

Hera's eyes narrowed on him. "Try your charm somewhere else, bloodsucker."

Rhys sent her a look of mock affront. "The judgment and prejudice. And from a witch, no less. You should know something about persecution."

Little sparks of energy flew through the air, colliding with Rhys. He jumped back and cursed.

"That's what you get for calling me a witch," Hera snarled.

I moved quickly, stepping between them. "Enough. Both of you, behave. And, King, lower the goddamned gun already."

"You'll vouch for him?" King pushed, arching a brow.

"Yes," I grumbled, sending Rhys a warning look. Vouching for his troublemaking ass meant anything he did would come back on me.

Kingston slowly lowered his weapon but didn't put it in one of his hidey-holes quite yet.

Rhys rolled his shoulders back. "That's a little better."

"What are you *really* doing here?" I asked. Rhys wouldn't come all the way across the country simply for shits and giggles. Unless he'd really reached a whole new level of boredom.

A smile stretched back across his face. "Your little mate wanted to know who your source was. So, here I am."

CHAPTER SEVENTEEN

Wren

I GAPED AT THE MERCURIAL MAN IN THE MIDDLE OF THE entryway, one with all sorts of opposing identities. "*You're* Ender's informant?"

"The one and only. With my fingers in all sorts of dark and dastardly pies." Rhys wiggled his fingers to accentuate the point.

I tried to identify each of his rings. One had an intricate tree carved into a circle as if it could serve as a seal. Another had a ragged mask that looked like something out of a nightmare. And on his pinky was a dark stone that looked like a black hole just waiting to swallow anyone it came into contact with.

"Keep all your fingers away from her," Puck snarled.

Rhys only beamed at him. "This is good. It's fun seeing your pack coming together in defense of a mate. I wasn't sure it would happen."

Something about Rhys's words set me on edge. Perhaps the

way they were spoken or the familiarity. Something about it didn't sit right. And I clearly wasn't the only one who felt that way.

Kingston bristled. "Why is he talking like he knows us?"

Ender sighed and squeezed the back of his neck. "Rhys has... some gifts."

"Excuse me," Rhys interjected. "Please don't talk about me like I'm some sort of party trick."

Even though the vampire spoke jokingly, I felt the undercurrent in the words, the weight of being different. And I understood it. I got the fear of people seeing you as a freak on a deep level. It tugged at me.

"Then tell us what they are," Hera pushed, wariness in her pale-green eyes.

Rhys sighed, reworking his hair into a knot atop his head. The mane was thick and tangled, dark brown with caramel-colored highlights woven throughout. The strands looked as if they'd been kissed by the sun, the same way his tan skin did.

None of it fit what I thought of when someone said *vampire*. There was no porcelain skin or blood-red lips. Rhys looked more like he was about to hike up a mountain than hide out from the sun. And he looked very much alive.

His ringed fingers drummed on his jeans-clad thigh. "A smidge of prophecy here and there, but also visions of the present."

It suddenly made sense how Ender was getting information about Red River without having an inside source. Wonder slid through me as I stared at Rhys. "You can focus your gifts on a specific target, can't you?"

I could do the same with my empath gifts, but it was difficult, and I definitely couldn't do it if I wasn't in the same room as my target.

Rhys shrugged. "Sometimes."

"You never had any contact with Red River, did you?" I pressed.

His nose wrinkled. "Consort with those animals? No insult intended. Never."

I turned to Ender. "Why the hell wouldn't you just tell me that? It would've put my mind at ease."

Rhys crossed his arms over his massive chest. "Yeah, End. Why didn't you just tell her that?"

"I'm going to kill you," Ender growled low.

Rhys just laughed. "This is going to be so much fun. I'm so glad I get a front-row seat."

"You think you're staying?" King challenged.

"Oh, yes. I'll be here for the long haul," Rhys said easily.

Locke scowled at him. "Because your psychic powers told you so?"

Rhys glanced Locke's way. "You're usually the nice one. Wake up on the wrong side of the bed today?"

"I don't like people I don't know sneaking onto our territory and putting our mate at risk," Locke snarled.

"Aaaaaah. I threatened your security genius. I get it. Sorry about that. But when I can see in my mind how you put the system in, it's fairly easy to beat it. Have you considered adding motion detectors with size-specific alerts so human-sized creatures trigger it but nothing else?"

Locke's jaw went slack. "That's—you—I—"

Rhys's grin was back. "Good idea, right? I'd go with the Excalibur system. They're less buggy than some of the other options. I'd be happy to help you install it. It's no problem at all. I like security."

"You should see his place. It's like walking a booby-trapped, landmine obstacle course," Brix muttered.

I glanced at him. "You know him, too?"

Brix shrugged. "He got us out of a sticky situation once."

"You mean I saved your life. You're welcome, by the way," Rhys huffed.

"Because I saved your life at least three times," Ender shot back.

"Poe-tay-toe, poe-tah-toe," Rhys singsonged.

Hera took another step forward, her eyes narrowing on the vampire. "If you are trying to screw us over—"

"I'm not," he clipped. "I'm here to help."

"If you're lying, I'll turn you into a frog. I can do it," Hera shot back.

Rhys's lips twitched. "I love it when you talk dirty to me."

Her nose wrinkled. "You aren't my type."

Rhys straightened his spine, suddenly looking far more affronted at that than at anything else our group had hurled at him. "Because I'm a vampire? Come on. I've got that wounded, bad-boy thing going for me. I'm *everyone's* type."

"Not unless you get rid of your dick," she bit out.

His jaw went slack, surprise lighting his amber eyes. "Oh, well. I guess that's okay. As long as you know that if you were into dicks, you'd be powerless against my charms."

"Keep telling yourself that, bloodsucker," Hera grumbled as she turned to walk out of the entryway.

"You'd be head over heels in love with me," Rhys called after her.

She just flipped him off.

"She would be," Rhys muttered.

Ender clapped a hand on his shoulder, turning him toward the back doors. "Come on, you and I need to have a talk."

"Can Wren come?" Rhys asked hopefully.

"No," Ender snapped.

"Always such a buzzkill."

CHAPTER EIGHTEEN

Ender

I KICKED MY FEET OUT AND TOOK A SWIG FROM THE WHISKEY bottle before handing it to Rhys. His nose wrinkled as he took it. "You couldn't be bothered with glasses?"

I sent him a droll look. "I hauled these two chairs out here so your delicate ass wouldn't have to sit on the ground. Isn't that enough?"

Rhys let out a huff. "So undignified." But he swallowed down a shot of whiskey. "At least you had the decency to bring the good stuff."

"What's the point in drinking anything else?" I stared out at the forest as the creek bubbled in front of us.

"This is your stewing spot. I recognize it."

I sent a glare in Rhys's direction. "Spying on me?"

"Can't help it," he muttered. "I've gotten partial to you staying alive."

"I do a pretty damn good job of that, so you can relax."

"Not lately," Rhys argued. "There have been a few too many close calls, and you've been asking me for too many favors."

My hackles rose at that. "If you don't want to help, then don't."

"That's not it, and you know it."

I huffed out a breath. "It's been coming from all sides lately. You fight off one attack, and another surfaces. Feels like there's nothing I can do to stop it."

Rhys was quiet for a long moment, the only sounds those of the creek and the animals darting through the forest. "You're more on edge than I've ever seen you. You're usually ice-cold, but you nearly bit my head off in there."

I knew he was right. Letting my temper or Rhys's goading get the best of me wasn't like me. I prized myself on my ability to blank every hint of expression from my face, never giving away what I cared about or who.

"You love her," Rhys said quietly.

I grabbed the bottle from him and took a healthy swig. The familiar burn lit down my throat, but I needed more. I wanted something that burned me from the inside out, something that would rival the emotional toll currently ravaging my system.

"I can't," I rasped.

"Ender…"

"I fucked up."

"We all do," Rhys assured me.

I shook my head and took another swig of the whiskey. "You don't get it. I was so damn cruel to her. And it wasn't just you I went to when I was looking into her. There were others. I'm why Bastian found her. Why she was tortured not once but twice. I called her a liar and a traitor. I accused her of working with that monster."

Rhys went quiet again, and I didn't blame him. It was a shitstorm of epic proportions. "You tell her you fucked up?"

"Yes, but—"

"You learn from it?"

My back teeth ground together. "It's complicated."

"You keep shutting her out, and all she wants is for you to let her in," Rhys surmised.

"Stop using your hocus-pocus on me," I bit out.

"I'm not. I just know you, End. And I know you don't want to let anyone close enough to hurt you. The only one who gets in your head is Brix, and that's only because of what you went through together."

I knew he was right, but I didn't have the first clue how to change it. I was who I was. The need to protect myself was practically in my DNA at this point.

Rhys grabbed the bottle and took another swig. "You want to soul-bond with someone, you have to let them in. You have to take that leap, knowing they will likely hurt you, but it'll also be worth it."

A burn lit along my sternum, but I shoved the sensation down. "And you're so good at that? I'm not the only one who's running."

Rhys's eyes flashed a brighter shade of gold. "Don't start. This isn't about me."

My molars clenched even harder because I knew he was right. I knew I had to figure out my bullshit. "I don't know if I can," I finally admitted.

"You're going to have to figure out a way. If you don't, you'll lose everything."

I stiffened, panic lighting through me. "You know something."

Rhys turned his gaze to the forest. "I'm here to make sure you all take the steps you need to take."

My panic grew because Rhys had called and steered me away from a certain course of action more than once, saving my life. So, if he was here telling me I needed to do certain things…I had to listen.

Rhys clapped his hands on his thighs before standing. "She's here. It'd be best if you two talked."

I saw no sign of Wren, scented nothing in the air, but a handful of seconds later, she appeared in the distance. As she approached, she studied the two of us carefully, her gaze finally holding on Rhys. "You don't need to leave on my account."

Rhys's mouth pulled into a charming smile, and he reached for her hand, bowing to brush his lips across the back of it.

A growl tore from my throat on instinct, and there was nothing I could do to hold it back. The idea of Rhys's mouth on Wren… His lips touching her. The urge to strike out and send him flying was almost more than I could take.

Rhys chuckled low in his throat, his eyes gleaming with amusement. He released Wren's hand and turned back to her. "Don't worry, we'll have plenty of time together. We start your training tomorrow."

Then, he was gone. And I was left alone with the one woman I'd done everything to avoid.

CHAPTER NINETEEN

Wren

I STARED AFTER THE MERCURIAL VAMPIRE, SO MANY QUESTIONS on the tip of my tongue. But, like usual, I had no answers. I looked back at Ender, who sat staring out at the forest. "What does he mean, training?"

Ender lifted a bottle to his lips and tipped it back. "With Rhys, you never know. But it's best to do exactly what he tells you."

Annoyance that flared to anger around the edges spread through me. It was always cryptic half-truths with Ender, and I was sick of it. "You trust him that blindly?"

His gaze flicked to me and held there for a moment, feeling like flames ghosting across my skin. "I do. He's saved my life more than once," Ender ground out.

Interest flared to life. I wanted to know more, wanted to know everything. Needed to find out what Rhys had saved Ender from and what his life had looked like before he became a part of the

Arcane pack. I tried easing into it, hoping I could tease information out of him over time if I did.

"How did you two meet?" I asked. When Ender didn't answer, I pressed a little more. "Vampires and wolf shifters aren't exactly known for being friends."

Ender's silence remained. He tipped the bottle to his lips again and kept staring at the forest.

Annoyance bled completely into anger, and I ripped the bottle from Ender's grasp. "Is it always going to be like this? Secrets and lies? Never sharing a damn thing because you think the worst of me?"

Ender's amber gaze slowly moved to me, locking on my face like a heat-seeking missile, and it didn't move away. Shadows swirled in his golden eyes, and a muscle twitched in his cheek. "I don't think the worst of you."

A scoff broke free from my throat.

Ender's eyes flashed pure gold, only making the shadows stand out more. "I think you're the most amazing creature I've ever met. You didn't let cruelty turn you dark. You got strong without stepping on the weak. And you leave goddamned miracles in your wake wherever you go."

Shock rocketed through me as I stared down at the man who'd been the cruelest. The one who'd doubted everything about me. The one who'd broken my heart. Who it turned out maybe didn't believe any of those lies anymore.

"Oh," I whispered. It was the only sound I could make. Barely even a word at all.

"Yeah," Ender muttered, grabbing the bottle and taking another swig.

"That was, um, nice of you." It was so juvenile and ridiculous to say, but I needed him to know I appreciated the words he'd spoken aloud. Because I knew it had cost him on some level.

Ender released some sort of derisive sound.

"What?" I asked, bristling.

"I'm not *nice,* Kitten."

"What you just said was," I challenged.

Ender looked up at me from his chair, his eyes growing colder. "I kill people, and I'm paid to do it."

"Bad people."

He shrugged, his gaze moving back to the forest as if it held all the necessary answers. "They're still marks on my soul. You should stay far away from me like you were doing before."

My annoyance was back, but something else pulled at me. My empathic gifts, I realized. Because they sensed the pain beneath Ender's words, the agony he covered with cruel barbs and by keeping his distance. So, I did the opposite. I moved closer.

"What if I don't want to stay far away?"

That amber gaze flicked up to me. At first glance, it appeared uncaring, as if Ender didn't give one damn if I jumped into the nearest river and got washed away. But I saw beneath it. Letting down my emotional shields for a single second, I felt it all.

A battle raged in him. Emotions warred for supremacy. Need and fear. Pain and pleasure. Love and hate.

"You should want to stay far away. Because when my resolve breaks, I'll fuck you so hard I'll imprint myself on your bones. You'll never be free of me. And you'll want to be. Because I'm destined for your nightmares, not your daydreams."

My heart hammered against my rib cage as my pulse thrummed in my neck. But I still stepped closer. And then closer still. Until I was standing between Ender's legs.

"What are you doing?" he rasped.

"Have you ever considered that maybe I want that? Want you? And whatever comes with it, dreams *and* nightmares? Because it's you, and you're meant for me."

My fingers hooked in the hem of my workout tank as my heart rate sped up. I sucked in a breath, searching for a moment of bravery, and then pulled the tank over my head and let it flutter to the forest floor.

CHAPTER TWENTY

Wren

My gaze stayed fixed on Ender's eyes as my heart raced, and my nipples pebbled in the cool afternoon air. I watched as those amber depths shifted and changed. Gold sparked in them as his pupils dilated.

Out of the corner of my eye, I saw Ender's fingers tighten around the bottle of whiskey and the arm of the chair. I felt the battle brewing within him as fur rippled over his forearms. "Walk. Away," he growled.

I jutted out my chin. "No."

I was done with these games. We needed something to break the cycle we were in. Moments of understanding followed quickly by a panicked retreat. We'd never move forward if stepping out was always followed by stepping back. And this was the only thing I could think of to break through.

Reckless? Yes. Dangerous? Quite possibly.

But I didn't give a damn. Because the way Ender was holding himself back from me was killing me slowly.

"Wren," he rasped. "My restraint is fraying."

"Good." I kicked off one shoe and then the other.

"Wren," Ender ground out in warning.

My fingers hooked in the band of my leggings, ignoring the tone in his voice. I slowly slid the spandex down my legs and kicked it off to the side. As I straightened, my confidence swelled. Because the rest of the guys had given me that. And more, I'd given it to myself.

My scarred skin was evidence of my strength and all I'd survived. My toned muscles were proof of all the work I'd put into building my strength so I'd be ready to fight. And I knew my eyes shone with need—a desire I was no longer hiding.

Ender could deal with it, or he could run.

"Kitten," he growled.

I didn't move.

He leaned forward in his chair, his hands hovering over my legs but not making contact. And then he scented the air as if memorizing the smell. "I don't deserve to touch this skin."

"Maybe, maybe not. But I want you to either way."

A low, rumbling sound emanated from Ender's chest, and his fingertips skated over my thighs. He closed his eyes and groaned. "Like warm silk, marked with your battle victories. I feel how strong you are. How fierce."

I shivered but didn't move.

Ender's fingers tracked higher. "Every line is a story your body tells." He opened his eyes and looked up into mine. "A story I'd give anything to know, and even more to ease."

Pressure built behind my eyes. I could take angry Ender. I could even take cruel Ender. But gentle Ender? That would kill me.

I lifted my hands as I moved in closer, sinking them into the hair piled on Ender's head in a knot. I gripped it hard, fascinated by how his eyes sparked as I did.

"Kitten," he growled.

"You promised me something."

More golden sparks danced across Ender's eyes. "You don't know what you're asking."

"Don't I?" I challenged. One hand tangled deeper in his hair, pulling tighter as my other grazed the shaved side of his head with my nails.

He let out a low snarl. "You want to play?"

"Yes," I breathed.

Ender moved so fast I didn't have a chance to brace. He cupped me at the apex of my thighs, hauling me closer to him. My back arched, pressing me into him, seeking more contact and friction.

"My little kitten's a greedy girl," he all but purred as I ground against his hand.

My mouth fell open, heat building between my legs.

And then his fingers parted me.

I sucked in a breath as two slid inside. I steadied myself on Ender's shoulder with one hand, my other still in his hair.

"Bend over," Ender ordered. "Give me one of those pretty nipples. I've been dying to know what you taste like."

My body obeyed before my mind had a chance to process the command. Maybe it was my wolf taking over, or maybe it was my nerve endings dying for more of Ender's touch. I didn't care. I simply wanted to give myself to whatever this was between us.

Ender's lips closed around the bud, pulling it deep into his mouth. My back arched, and a moan slipped free. Ender's tongue swirled around the hard peak, pulling it tauter as his fingers mirrored the motion inside me.

"Give me more," he growled around my nipple. "Let me stretch you so you're ready for me to truly take you. Soak my hand and come on my fingers."

My body moved like an instrument, and he was the conductor.

Building crescendos and easing decrescendos. Every time I got close, Ender sensed it and backed off.

It was my turn to let out a growl as the swirl of his fingers slowed. I gripped his hair tighter, pulling him back from my breast, my eyes flashing to wolf.

Ender let out a low chuckle. "Need something?"

"Yes," I ground out.

"Tell me," he challenged.

"Make me come."

A smile tugged at his lips. "My fucking pleasure."

Ender's fingers swirled wider as they thrust in and out. The stretch was almost painful but not quite. My legs began to tremble, and my eyes fluttered closed.

"Don't," he snapped. "Eyes on me. I don't want to lose a second of that turquoise. Need to see how they darken when you shatter."

My walls fluttered around his fingers as he pumped them in and out of me.

"That's my girl, my vicious kitten. Show me how beautifully you come for me. Show me you're ready to take me."

His words sent me over the edge, the orgasm crashing into me. I struggled to stay on my feet as wave after wave hit me, struggled to keep my eyes on Ender, but his wonder held me captive. His reverence.

He led me through every last peak and valley until he pulled his fingers from me. Then he stood, forcing me back a step but never losing my eyes before licking his fingers clean. It was then that his eyes closed. "Everything I dreamed of."

Ender's eyes were pure gold when they reopened. Pure fire. Pure need. "Hands on the chair, Kitten."

A shiver racked my body, but I was already moving, bending and gripping the chair resting against the tree.

I heard the sound of a zipper. Shuffling. Every part of me stood at attention.

"Look at my beautiful kitten. Ass on display. Pussy dripping. Last chance. Want to run, Kitten?"

My mouth went dry as a new rush of wetness flooded my thighs. "Not running anywhere."

"Don't say I didn't warn you," he growled.

And he was right. There was no warning. No easing in with Ender. He gripped my hips and took. Slamming into me so hard my eyes watered.

But it was *him*. And that made it beautiful.

Raw, feral need. As if Ender were bleeding out every tortured moment that had shored up between us. He took and released, over and over. The sheer power of all he was had my legs trembling and walls fluttering.

"Not yet," Ender snarled. He fisted his hand in my hair, pulling it tight and forcing me to hold on, to fight back the final crest.

He thrust in, impossibly deeper, hitting a spot that had tears springing free. "Let go," he ordered.

And I did.

The force of the orgasm had my vision tunneling and darkness threatening to overtake me, but I fought it back, just like I fought for Ender to let me in. I gave as good as I got, meeting him thrust for thrust as he came. He released so deep inside me that it only sent me tumbling anew. But I wanted it all. Everything he had to give.

His thrusts started to slow, his breathing becoming ragged as one last wave hit me—so much pleasure it was almost painful now. I fought to stay standing. As if he sensed it, Ender wrapped an arm around my stomach and pulled me upright. I felt his chest heave against my back, his dick still twitching inside me as I struggled to catch my breath.

For the first time, I felt like I'd gotten the real Ender. No holding back. No walls. Simply him.

As he slid from my body, I winced, the pain at the loss of him, the tender aftermath of what we'd shared. Ender stiffened. "I'm sorry. I—"

I whirled on him. "Don't you dare. I wanted this. I gave as good as I got, so pull your head out of your ass and stop pushing me away."

One corner of Ender's mouth kicked up. "Okay."

"Okay?" I parroted, shock racing through me.

"Okay, Kitten." He brushed his lips across mine. And then he pulled his T-shirt over his head and put it on me, gently sliding one arm through one sleeve and then the other.

I watched as he pulled his pants back on and slid his feet into his shoes, then he brushed the hair out of my face and tucked it behind my ear. He kissed me again. "I'm going to be so bad at this," he warned.

"Better than not trying at all," I whispered.

"I hope you're right."

A throat cleared, and we both whirled to find Brix grinning at us. "I'm going to take it that this means you two are starting to figure your shit out?"

CHAPTER TWENTY-ONE

Brix

I SCENTED SEX IN THE AIR, AND MY WOLF PRESSED AT MY SKIN. He wanted in on the fun, but he was also…happy. And more than a little relieved, just like my human half. Because Ender and Wren needed this.

There were times you had to let your animal side lead. Move through the world on instinct instead of using reason. And their human halves had been getting in the way far too much.

"Fuck off," Ender grumbled.

I just grinned wider. "What? I can't be happy for my best friend and my girl?"

End shook his head. "When did you become some mushy Cupid?"

I shrugged. "Since I found out what it was like to be truly happy."

Ender and Wren stilled. Wren's expression went soft as she looked at me—so much tenderness there. Sadness filled Ender's gaze, and I knew why. He was thinking about all we'd lost and everything we'd had to overcome. But that sadness was equally matched by a beautiful relief. The kind that saw just how much had been healed in me.

But, of course, he had to cover that. He straightened. "I'm going to kick the crap out of Rhys for a while. This is way too fucking mushy for me."

He took off toward the house, and Wren started to laugh. She looked at me, the amusement in her eyes deepening and warming. "Is he always this grumpy when he catches feelings?"

I thought about it for a moment. "Honestly, I don't know. He never has before."

Wren's spine straightened, and her jaw went slack. "Seriously?"

I shook my head as I moved to find the rest of her discarded clothes. "Nope. He's never let anyone close enough for that to happen."

"It makes me a little sad," she said softly. "I know I should be all possessive, but I can't help but feel for how lonely he must've been."

Grabbing Wren's leggings, top, and shoes, I moved in her direction and dropped a kiss to the top of her head. "My little empath."

"I guess I'm always going to think about how something like this makes him feel."

I dropped to my knees and began sliding one of Wren's legs into the leggings, relishing the feeling of her skin and how the bond between us flared to life at the contact. "What happened when we were young messed with us. We lost everyone we cared about except for each other."

Wren placed her hands on my shoulders to steady herself. "I'm so sorry, Brix. I—"

"It wasn't you."

She pulled the corner of her lip between her teeth. "I know, but he's a part of me. And he's put you all through so much. I know you don't blame me, but it's sometimes hard to reconcile it all."

I gently moved her second foot into the workout pants and

slowly began pulling them up. Something about the act of dressing her felt like caretaking in a way, drawing us closer together and giving me something to do when so much was out of my control. When her leggings were in place, I lifted Ender's tee and kissed Wren's belly. I kept my lips there, hovering against her skin as I spoke. "You've burned him out of you, Little Warrior. Through every act of kindness and care. There's none of him in you anymore."

She pulled back, her fingers tightening on my shoulders. "Is that really what you think?"

I looked up into those beautiful, turquoise eyes. "It's what I know."

One of Wren's hands moved from my shoulder to my cheek, her fingers ghosting over it in soothing strokes. "And how are you doing with everything going on?"

My gaze dipped, focusing on a new task. I took my time unlacing one of Wren's sneakers and slipping it onto her foot. She didn't rush my answer as if she knew I needed time to find the words. "I'm edgy," I finally admitted. "My wolf wants you with us at all times."

"And your human half?"

"I want that, too, but I also recognize that it might not be the healthiest urge." I tied the laces of the first shoe in a perfect bow and then went to work on the second.

"It's never good when our wolves are at odds with the rest of us," Wren said softly.

My jaw worked back and forth as I slid Wren's second sneaker on. I didn't want to say the next part because I knew it would hurt her, even if it shouldn't. But I also knew that holding back wouldn't get us anywhere. So, I kept focused on the shoe as I spoke. "I've been having dreams."

Wren's hands sifted into my hair, coaxing my gaze up to her face. There was so much tenderness and understanding there. "Will you tell me?"

My throat worked as I struggled to swallow. "It's about the

attack when I was younger. I'm back there. But, sometimes, instead of my sister…it's you."

Wren only stilled for a moment. Then she moved, sinking to her knees so we were face-to-face. She wrapped her arms around me and nuzzled in. "I'm right here. I'm not going anywhere."

I breathed her in, reminding myself of exactly what she'd said. She was here. Alive. Heart beating against my chest. And we were doing everything we could to keep her safe.

"What can I do?" she whispered.

It meant something that she asked. She didn't assume or demand. She wanted to know what I thought I needed.

I pulled back, my hand sliding along her jaw. "Ink me."

CHAPTER TWENTY-TWO

Wren

I felt the surprise flare in my eyes at Brix's words. *Ink me.* "I don't know how." But even as I said it, the ache in my chest deepened. Even without releasing my emotional shields, I could feel his pain, his fear.

"I can teach you," he murmured, his thumb tracing my lower lip.

"Can you explain it to me?" I asked gently. "What it will give you."

I worried that it might be the search for more pain. The release he used to find through sparring or ink sessions with Ender. I knew that had gotten him through some of his darkest times. But I didn't want to be another source of pain for him.

Brix's hand slid into my hair. "I need to feel you in the dark."

I frowned, trying to understand.

"I've carved the darkness into my skin, over and over again, but now I need the light." He traced a scene of two wolves in battle, snarling at each other.

"But there's no room," I said, confused. The truth was, most of Brix's skin was covered in tattoos. There was very little space to add anything.

"There's an enchanted ink that's metallic in nature. I want you to paint the light in the dark. I don't want to erase the images. I want to bring balance."

I suddenly understood because I'd experienced the same. Looking back on my past, it wasn't that I wanted to live through it again, but I could appreciate it for what it had taught me and where it had brought me. It had made me strong and given me the life I now had—the guys, our home. The darkness was only that because of the light it held—a light that had carried me through.

I leaned forward on my knees and brushed my lips against Brix's. "I'll remind you of the light."

His shoulders relaxed as he pulled me into him and stood. "I love you, Little Warrior."

"I love you, too."

Brix lifted me, and my legs encircled his waist. He gave my ass a little love tap as he carried me inside and toward the tattoo room. "You know, this is a lot of power in your hands."

I grinned. "I could put hearts and butterflies all over your badass ink."

He chuckled. "They'd still be badass butterflies."

My grin widened against Brix's neck, the feeling of his skin and the scent of leather and spice heating my blood. He was unending comfort and scorching heat all at once. I could feel the darkness raking at my emotional shields, but I didn't let it scare or overwhelm me. We were going to deal with it in our own way. In a way that wouldn't drown me or overtake Brix.

Voices sounded from various areas of the house, but we didn't see a single soul on the way to the tattoo studio. When we reached it, Brix flipped on the light and gently set me down.

"You know," I said, looking around the space for the second time and taking in new details, "I could get used to you carrying me everywhere."

Brix chuckled as he moved to a sink and began washing his hands. "Don't tempt me, Little Warrior. I'll take you against me any time I can get it."

I pressed my thighs together, trying to alleviate some of the tension there. Brix's gaze dropped to them, not missing a thing. "Killing me, Little Warrior. Killing me."

I cleared my throat and moved to the sink, too. "I'm pulling it together. I can be a professional."

Brix pressed a kiss to my temple as I washed my hands. "It's good to know it's a struggle for you, too."

I tipped my head back as I dried my hands, then kissed him. The taste of his heady spice filled my mouth, and I moaned softly. What had gotten into me? I couldn't seem to stop touching, tasting, and drowning in my mates. I could never get enough.

It was Brix who finally broke the kiss, his breathing labored. "Ink," he growled.

"Right," I mumbled, clasping my hands in front of me as if that would stop my horny self.

But as Brix moved around the room, gathering supplies, a different sort of fascination took over. He was so at home in the space. Had a quiet confidence that was hypnotizing. He gathered something that looked like some kind of gun, some wrapped needles, and two small pots.

"Tattooing supernaturals is different than humans," Brix explained.

"Because we heal so fast?" I asked, remembering how the tattoo Brix had given me had healed almost instantly.

"That's part of it, but you also have to use special ink to make sure it's permanent. Because our bodies will disintegrate normal tattoo ink."

I moved in closer, studying the pot of ink. It looked like pure shimmer—not like diamonds, but even more sparkly, as if it were fairy dust. "This is different than what you tattooed me with."

Brix lifted the small pot for me to see. "It's light ink. Enchanted to be used on the darkest tattoos."

The ink itself was hypnotizing, as if it could pull me in and swallow me whole. And as I touched the pot, I could feel the magic humming there. "Powerful," I whispered.

"Yes. Especially with you wielding it," Brix said softly.

He walked me through the basics, explaining that there were different types of needles, but I'd be using the finest one for this. "Don't worry, you won't hurt me," he said as he pulled off his T-shirt.

I took in all the images inked across his skin—ones that seemed to expose his worst nightmares but also his greatest loyalties. *Arcane* was inked over his left pec with five paw prints below it. His pack. On his right were three paw prints, each hollowed out. My heart ached when I realized they were for the family he'd lost.

Another battle scene was in the center of his chest, but this one was full of nonsensical monsters, dark and disturbing. This. *This* was where he needed the light.

I lifted the tattoo machine with my gloved hand. Taking a breath, I looked up into Brix's eyes. "You're sure?"

"I trust you."

The ache in my chest intensified, but I knew he needed this. Closing my hand over the machine, it buzzed to life. I focused on one monster in particular. It was part shape, part smoke, its mouth open in a silent scream. But the scream was sucking out the soul of its enemy, taking its very essence.

I touched the needle to Brix's skin, etching a line along the monster, and then pulled my hand back. I watched as the ink seeped into his flesh and the tattoo changed. The shimmer danced across the beast, and instead of being in battle with another creature, its head tipped back, arm-like appendages reaching skyward as if it were searching for salvation instead of attack.

"How?" I croaked.

"The ink takes what's in our minds—yours and mine—and transforms the tattoo into what we need most."

I stared in wonder at Brix's chest, the designs pulling me back in. I lost track of time as I worked, letting instinct guide me until my arm ached and I had to put the tattoo machine down. But as I stepped back, I took in everything on Brix's torso. Some battles still remained, a reminder of his strength, but the stories they told were now ones of hope.

He slid off the chair and moved to the large mirror on the room's far wall, taking me with him. Brix stared at his reflection in the mirror, hypnotized by the new images gracing his skin. Then, he turned, his hands sliding into my hair and his mouth taking mine. "I love you, Little Warrior. You make everything better."

"You're being mushy in our tattoo studio?" Ender barked, cutting into my haze of happiness. "Is not one place sacred?"

I struggled not to laugh as I turned in Brix's arms. "Got a problem, Mr. Pussy Palace?"

"Pussy Palace?" Rhys asked, striding in behind him. "There's gotta be a story there."

"There's not," Ender clipped.

I looked up at Brix. "Told you catching feelings made him grumpy."

CHAPTER TWENTY-THREE

Wren

THE DIN OF THE LUNCHTIME RUSH AT THE NEWLY renovated Arcane washed over me, covering me like a comforting blanket. The guys hadn't been thrilled about the idea of me returning to work, but after the intensity of the past few weeks, I needed the routine and normalcy. The agreement was that I'd have at least a two-person team with me at all times.

Today, that team was Puck and Rhys—a Rhys who apparently hadn't experienced small-town life or bar-food fare, because he seemed enchanted by every new discovery. "Beer-battered french fries," he muttered, staring at the slice of potato. "Where have these been all my life?"

Puck chuckled as he poured two beers for me to take to a table of regulars. "Who knew all it took for you to behave was a bucket of fries?"

Rhys popped a fry into his mouth. "I'm very open to bribery."

Puck set the two beers on my tray as his gaze slid over my face. "You feeling okay? This isn't too much?"

"I'm good. I promise," I said, taking the beers to the table and checking their waters. As I turned back, it was to find Rhys kissing a very flustered Dina's hand.

"It is such a pleasure to meet you, Dina."

"Who is this?" she growled at Puck. "And why are his lips on my hand?"

Puck just started laughing. "Dina, Rhys. Rhys, Dina. And you might want to let her go because she's got a bat back here, and she's not afraid to use it."

Rhys's brows rose. "A fighter. I like it."

Dina tugged her hand free and turned to me. "Who is this? Really."

My lips twitched. "He's a friend of Ender's who's visiting."

That had her eyes narrowing. "That moody bastard doesn't have any friends."

Rhys barked out a laugh. "Truer words have never been spoken. We're more…life-debt bonded," he explained.

Dina leaned in, grabbing my hand. "Is everything okay? Is your dad back?"

With Clyde's help, we'd explained to her what was going on, and she'd handled it better than expected, saying she'd known something was up with the guys. She'd just thought they were CIA, not wolf shifters.

"I'm good. Rhys is just here for, uh, backup," I said.

"I am not *backup*," Rhys huffed. "I am a first line of defense. Please and thank you."

The front door opened, and Clyde strode in, followed by Franco and Juan. He beamed the moment he saw Dina. "There's my girl."

Her cheeks flushed. "Don't you start."

Clyde just grinned wider. "What? I can't say that you look stunning today?"

Dina just glared at him, and I couldn't help but laugh.

"Get it, boss man," Juan called as he moved toward the bar. "Those sweet nothings are panty droppers."

Dina's glare grew more heated as she turned it on Juan. "You talk about my panties one more time, and I'm takin' that bat to the side of your head."

Franco clapped a hand on Juan's shoulder. "Don't worry, Dina. I'll keep him in line."

She let out a scoff. "No one can do that."

I moved behind the bar and pulled out my order pad. "Guys, meet Ender's friend, Rhys. Rhys, this is Juan, Franco, and Clyde. They are all part of Crescent Kingdom, in various capacities."

Juan's eyes narrowed as he studied Rhys, and then he leaned across the bar to me and dropped his voice to a whisper. "What is he? A wolf? A witch? A banshee? A minotaur?"

I struggled not to laugh.

Franco rolled his eyes. "He's been hitting Google a little too hard."

Rhys arched a brow as he studied the three humans. "They know about our world?"

Puck grimaced. "Some shit went down."

"And you trust them?" Rhys pressed.

Clyde bristled at that. "We'd do anything to protect Wren, and the guys are our brothers."

Rhys grinned. "Good. We'll need you."

"Dude," Juan said, leaning closer. "What are you? I don't get a wolfy vibe."

Rhys's nose wrinkled. "As if. I'm what you would call a vampire."

Juan's eyes went comically wide. "Like…you want to drink my blood? That kind of vampire?"

Rhys chuckled and reached for his whiskey. "Not yours in particular, no."

Juan straightened on his stool, suddenly looking affronted.

"What's wrong with my blood? It's good blood. Probably the best blood ever."

"Jesus," Franco muttered.

Puck wrapped an arm around me, leaning his head against mine. "Tell me again why we needed to share with this idiot."

Rhys set down his glass and turned on his stool so he faced the human contingent. "Taking blood from the vein is an intimate experience. It bonds the two creatures in a way. And since I'm not particularly taken with you in that way, I'm not going to rip out your carotid."

Franco looked on stunned, but Juan just looked thoughtful. "So…what?" Juan asked. "You drink out of blood bags? Or blood cans like on *True Blood*? I fucking loved that show."

Rhys chuckled. "Something like that."

Clyde put a hand over his neck. "Just keep any sharp teeth away from my veins."

"How about we focus on human food?" I suggested, tapping my order pad. "What can I get you?"

The guys ordered, and I got lost in the hustle and bustle of the lunch rush again. Our human friends seemed to hit it off with Rhys after a few moments of nerves, and they shot the shit about all things small-town and supernatural, each side fascinated by the other.

As I cleared away the plates, I took stock of the overflowing recycling bin. I ditched the plates in the kitchen for Gary and moved to empty the bin.

"Don't even think about it," Puck called. "I'll do it after I finish these drinks."

"I can empty the trash," I shot back.

"Not alone, you can't," he clipped, his green eyes turning hard.

I tried not to let annoyance get the best of me. "Fine."

Rhys slid off his stool. "I will escort the little vixen."

Puck's eyes narrowed on him. "You've been downing whiskeys all afternoon."

Rhys executed what resembled a bastardized version of a sobriety field test and ended in a tap dance number. "I'm good, see?"

Dina hollered at Puck for two more drinks, and he let out a growl. "Fine. But you stick to her like white on rice."

Rhys saluted Puck. "I'm on duty."

I rolled my eyes at them and hoisted the recycling bin into my arms.

"I can get that," Rhys offered.

"I'm good, but you can get the door," I called around the side of the bin.

"At your service." Rhys hurried ahead, opened the back door, and held it wide.

I shuffled out toward the recycling, but only made it three steps before a hand fisted in my hair, yanking me to the side.

"It's about time, you little bitch."

CHAPTER TWENTY-FOUR

Wren

THE BIN I HELD TUMBLED OUT OF MY ARMS AS THE HOLD on my hair tightened, and my whole body was jerked to the side. Glass shattered, cans clattered, and the bin itself flew to the ground.

I moved on instinct, my elbow flying back into my attacker's gut. He grunted, and his hold on my hair loosened just enough for me to pull free. I whirled, hands moving in front of my face into a defensive position.

The man cursed, pulling a blade from his pocket. It was then that I really took him in: longish, stringy hair that looked unwashed, dirty clothes, brown eyes with pupils the size of pinpricks.

It wasn't Bastian or one of his men. It wasn't anyone associated with Red River. Instead, it was someone else from my past. The one member of the Death Walkers MC who'd managed to escape Brix's wrath. Their second-in-command, Dent.

He sneered at me as he flicked out his blade. "You ruined everything, you cunt. And now you're gonna feel that pain."

Dent lunged forward, but I quickly dodged to the side, pulling my own blade from my back pocket. I felt the carving in the handle, *KINGSTON* in intricate letters, press into my palm. It was the same blade that had saved my life with Marcelle.

There was trust in that. A belief that the weapon would carry me through because it had before.

Dent let out a sound that was something between a snort and a scoff. "You think you can go up against me? That knife isn't going to protect you."

"We'll see about that," I muttered as I dodged another of his blows.

Dent spun, swiping his blade through the air. He was quicker than he should've been and more forceful, too. It was almost beyond human strength.

And then I saw his eyes again. I remembered what all the Death Walkers were mixed up in. Human trafficking. Drugs. If Dent was on amphetamines, it could make him a match for my shifter strength.

I cursed as his blade swiped again, this time catching me across the forearm. Pain bloomed, but I managed to land an answering kick that sent Dent stumbling back several steps.

His eyes widened and then narrowed again. "You're one of them. Some mutant freak. Aren't you?"

"I'm something you never should've crossed." Memories of my time in their hold flashed in my mind. The agony of their torture. The cruelty of their words.

Dent let out a low, ugly laugh. "I'm going to enjoy killing you. Bleeding every ounce of blood from your body. Feeling your breaths slow and then stop altogether. I just wish I had more time, endless hours to make you feel every ounce of pain possible."

Dent charged then. I slowed my breathing, letting my wolf take the lead. My shifter vision let me see the attack before it landed, the arc his arm would take, the trajectory of the blade. I slipped under the blow, my knife following through and landing square between his shoulder blades before stumbling forward.

A choking sound emanated from Dent as he started to fall. He twisted, his eyes wide in shock as he clawed at his neck, his blade clattering to the cement. I must've gotten his airway.

Panic filled his brown eyes, and he made a gurgling sound. I leaned over him, getting close. "You should've run when you had the chance."

Dent's eyes widened again, and I saw so much fear there. But I didn't let it stop me. I called on my wolf, letting claws lengthen from my fingertips. And then I plunged my hand into his chest and tore out his heart.

Everything stilled in the human. Wide eyes. Stark-white face. Mouth open.

And then, there was nothing at all.

It was more kindness than he had ever shown me. A quicker death than he deserved. But I wouldn't become like the monsters who haunted me.

Dropping the heart to the pavement, I wiped my hand clean on the man's shirt and straightened.

Rhys stood there, arms crossed over his chest. "We really need to work on your technique."

I gaped at the vampire. "I could've used a little help."

He simply shrugged. "I needed to see where your battle skills were at. Not in some sparring ring, but in real time."

A sick feeling swept over me. "Did you know he was here?"

Rhys plucked a piece of invisible lint off his shirt. "I might've seen an altercation taking place in a vision."

"You what?" a new voice snarled. Puck prowled through the back door and headed toward Rhys. "You *knew* she was going to be attacked, and you did nothing?"

Rhys held up a hand. "Just relax, I—"

"Relax?" Puck bit out. "I'm going to fucking kill you."

CHAPTER TWENTY-FIVE

Puck

Rage like I'd felt only a handful of times in my life swept through me like a wildfire tearing down a forest. The night I'd realized my brother had betrayed me. Alice, too. When we got that video of Wren, the Death Walkers torturing her. And when Bastian took her.

But this…? Rhys had been a guest in our home. He'd promised to protect Wren. Instead, he'd stood out here as if he were watching an experiment take place. Maybe that was all this was to him. Curiosity.

Not to us. To me. To me, Wren was everything. Savior and peace. Understanding and my ultimate resting place. She was simply…my soul's missing piece. And Rhys could've let her be ripped from this earth. And for what? To see how good her fighting was?

A snarl tore from my throat, and I charged, launching myself into the air and coming down with a hard right hook to Rhys's jaw.

His head snapped back as Wren yelled at me to stop. A second later, she threw herself at me.

It was a risky play with my wolf this riled, but Birdie was smart as hell. Instead of hitting Rhys with another blow, I caught her in my arms. Her legs went around my waist, her arms around my neck, and she held on for dear life. "Don't," she rasped. "It's not worth it."

"Isn't it?" I growled. "He could've gotten you killed."

Rhys moved his jaw back and forth, a cracking sound coming from the bones. "I wouldn't have let it get that far. But I needed to see where her skills stood." He let out a huff. "She needs some work."

Wren dropped from me and stalked toward him. "Work, huh?"

Rhys's shoulders straightened. "Yes. You need to be more at one with your wolf. She'll help your reaction time and—"

Wren's fist lashed out, lightning-quick, smashing into the other side of Rhys's jaw.

"Goddamn it!" he howled, clutching his face. "I might be immortal, but that fucking hurt."

Wren simply grinned. "How's that for reaction time?"

Rhys scowled at her as he straightened. "I guess I deserved that."

"Damn right, you did," I snapped, moving to Wren and wrapping an arm around her. I needed to feel her, each inhale, the beat of her heart. Panic clawed at me. There'd been too many close calls, and I felt like I was holding my sanity together with duct tape and a prayer.

Rhys huffed out a breath. "The enemy has been dispatched, and my visions tell me he was the last of the Death Walkers." He straightened his jacket. "What an overly dramatic name for a human bike group."

Wren's lips twitched. "Bike group?"

"Is that not what they do? Ride around on their little bikes?" Rhys asked.

I let out a grunt. "Bikers. They're called bikers. And they're a motorcycle club."

"Whatever," Rhys muttered. "They know nothing of what it means to walk the veil between life and death."

My eyes narrowed on him. There was something there. Vampires walked that line every day, but this was something more.

"Holy shit," a new voice muttered. "Clean up on aisle eight." Juan's eyes were wide with shock and a bit of awe. He looked at Rhys. "Did you do this?"

Rhys shook his head and gestured to Wren. "The lady here took out the trash."

Juan's gaze snapped to Wren as Clyde and Franco moved into the alley behind him. "Dude, you are a badass."

Wren chuckled. "Thanks?"

"Is that his heart?" Franco asked, looking a little green.

She grimaced. "Sorry. It was necessary." Her gaze flicked to Rhys. "Doesn't this bother you? All the blood?"

Rhys shook his head. "I don't drink human blood."

My jaw went slack. "At all?"

A muscle fluttered in the vampire's cheek. "No. Think of it as me being a vegetarian."

"So, what? You live off bunnies and stuff?" Juan asked.

"Something like that." Rhys turned to the body. "We need to dispose of this. Any ideas?"

"We got it," Clyde said, ambling forward. "There's a fast-moving river a few miles out of town where we can dump him."

"This is my mess," Wren began.

"Girlie," Clyde said, pinning her with a stare. "We said we had your back. Let us have it. Now, get back inside so you gots an alibi."

I squeezed her shoulder. "It's not a bad idea."

It wasn't just the supernatural world we needed to worry about. If the sheriff got wind of a murder, that could be a whole other sort of trouble. The panic was back, clawing at me. The need to get Wren back onto pack land where I could keep her safe pushed at me.

I did my best to breathe through it, but I couldn't get myself to let Wren go. Her head tilted back, and she studied me carefully. "Are you okay?"

I jerked my head in a nod. "Fine."

Little worry lines were carved into the spot between Wren's brows. "Puck—"

"Let's just get through today, okay?"

She was quiet but didn't look away, her gaze peeling back layer after layer.

I dropped my forehead to hers and breathed in the scent of wildflowers and rain. "We've got threats coming from all sides. My wolf's on edge. And we're both freaking the fuck out that we won't be able to protect you." And there was more. More I wasn't ready to share. But this was enough. For now.

Wren's fingers fisted in my shirt. "I'm fine. Look, I protected myself. And we'll figure the rest out. One thing at a time. As long as we're together, we can tackle anything."

I wanted to believe her. More than anything, I wanted to believe that we would all make it through. But I wasn't so sure she was right.

CHAPTER TWENTY-SIX

Wren

I kept a close eye on Puck all afternoon. The moment we came back inside, he'd donned his mask. The one of the flirty charmer. He'd laid it on thick for Ginger when she and Amos came in for date night and had gone above and beyond slinging drinks and chatting up everyone in the bar. Everyone except for me.

Annoyance and worry battled within me as I felt the distance growing. And it sure as hell didn't help that Rhys watched the whole thing like he was taking in a tennis match. By the time our replacements came in for the dinner shift, I was cranky and more than a little pissed off.

Normally, Puck wouldn't have let that stand. He would've pressed to know what was bothering me. Instead, he remained completely silent as he drove Rhys and me home.

Rhys leaned forward from the back seat, his focus moving between us like that tennis match was back in action. "Am I the only one feeling the awkwardness?"

"You're lucky you're not feeling my hand ripping out your heart," Puck muttered as he hit a button to open the gate onto Arcane territory.

I turned toward the window, watching the familiar trees pass as the road curved toward the house. It only took a handful of minutes, but it felt like an eternity. The moment Puck slowed the SUV, I was out and heading for the house. As soon as I hauled the door open, the other guys and Hera were there.

Kingston looked particularly surly. "Puck said something happened. What?" he growled.

Locke moved into my space, his hand cupping my face as he swept my body to make sure I wasn't injured. "You're okay?"

"I'm totally fine," I assured him.

"Then why," Ender snarled, struggling to keep his breathing even, "is there a healing blade mark on your arm?"

A series of growls lit the air, and Brix moved to lift my arm for inspection. "This looks like it was deep."

"Barely a scratch," Rhys huffed.

"A deep wound because *you* wanted to conduct some sick experiment," Puck snapped.

All eyes moved to Rhys, but Ender prowled toward him. "Tell me you didn't."

"She was perfectly safe," Rhys defended. "I would've stepped in if things had gotten out of hand."

"The fuck you would've. You knew Dent was out there. Knew he would try to kill Wren. You told me you had her back, but you're a goddamned liar," Puck snarled.

Kingston moved so quickly Rhys didn't have a prayer of defense. His fist lashed out, striking Rhys square in the nose with a sickening crunch.

Rhys doubled over, cupping his face. "Damn it all to hell. You broke it."

"You deserve far worse. You asked for our trust and betrayed it the first chance you got," Kingston ground out. "You're lucky I didn't take your head."

I crossed to King and placed a hand on his arm. "That's taking it a little far. He really was trying to assess my fighting skills."

"I don't give a damn," Kingston roared. "You could've been seriously hurt. Killed." He hauled me against him, his breaths ragged.

I wrapped my arms around his waist, giving him what he needed. Contact. The assurance that I was all right.

"I need some air," Puck muttered, heading back out the door.

My eyes followed him as he left, but I kept a hold of King. It was as if I were being pulled in infinite directions because we were all falling apart.

Rhys straightened and cracked his nose back into place. He let out a stream of curses at the fresh wave of pain.

I met his gaze with a pointed stare. "You did deserve that one."

Ender snickered. "At least it wasn't my nose for once."

"I can remedy that," Rhys challenged.

I released my hold on King and looked up into his eyes. "Are you okay?"

His hands ghosted over my face. "I'm all right." He brushed his lips over mine. "Can't stand the thought of you being hurt in any way."

"I feel the same about you." The idea that any of them could be injured because of some danger I'd put them in was almost more than I could take.

Kingston kissed me again. "We'll get through it together."

"Together," I whispered, glancing over my shoulder at the still wide-open door.

"Go," King said softly. "He needs you."

I looked up at our alpha, searching his pale-blue gaze. "You're sure?"

He nodded and then kissed my forehead. "Go. We've got things handled here."

I didn't wait. I took off at a jog out the door, hoping that having things *handled* didn't mean a group beatdown of Rhys. I scented the air and followed the trail of smoky whiskey. Puck had put some serious distance between him and the house, but I finally found him about a mile away. He'd followed the creek's path and stood staring at the bubbling water in the twilight.

His blond hair caught the purplish light, making it almost glow. But as I approached, his muscles stiffened. "I need some time, Wren."

Wren. Not Birdie, like he usually called me. It was as if he was creating an invisible distance between us.

"Not leaving you alone when you're hurting," I said softly.

The tension flowing through Puck twisted his muscles tighter. One second, he stood before me as a man. The next, a golden wolf was bounding away.

I cursed, instantly letting my wolf free. She gladly accepted the challenge, but our shift wasn't as quick as Puck's. We could make up for that with our speed on the ground. That was the thing about growing up as a submissive. You got fast.

My paws hit the forest floor in a thundering beat as I chased Puck's trail. It wasn't long before I caught him in my sights, a flash of gold in the darkening woods.

I pushed harder, my muscles burning and my lungs heaving, but I gained. His smoky whiskey scent grew stronger, and it was the fuel I needed.

With one last push, I launched myself into the air. I caught Puck on the fly, the force of my leap taking us both to the ground in a roll. We landed just beside the creek on a mossy embankment.

I didn't wait. My teeth pressed to the side of Puck's neck, pressure without puncture. But I'd bite if I needed to.

Puck let out a low, frustrated growl. But then he shifted back to his human form, and a completely naked man was underneath me.

CHAPTER TWENTY-SEVEN

Wren

I TRIED NOT TO LET THE GOLDEN SKIN AND TAN BODY distract me. My teeth stayed right at Puck's very human neck as I growled.

Puck simply chuckled. "You got me. Shift." His hands sifted through my fur as if wooing my human half back.

I was tempted to bite him just for the hell of it, but I still needed my human half to communicate with the bastard, so I began my shift. I felt the telltale pop and crack of bones, and before long, I was straddling Puck in my human form.

His green eyes flashed in the dark, his hands moving to cup my breasts. I smacked them away. "You haven't earned that," I growled.

"Birdie," he cooed as if that would make me melt. "I need to feel you. Lose myself in you."

I understood the urge. The physical was sometimes so much easier. A way to forget everything around you. But that wasn't what we needed right now.

Grabbing Puck's wrists, I held them over his head. He grinned. "Kinky. I like it."

I let out a low growl. "I will bite you."

"I'm into it." He nipped my bottom lip.

"Not in a fun way," I gritted out.

Puck pushed up, trying to kiss me.

"Don't." The single word cracked out like a whip as I released Puck's hands and sat up.

"Birdie," he whispered, losing the amusement.

"Tell me what's going on," I begged. That mask started to rise again, and pain flooded my system. My hands moved to Puck's stubbled cheeks. "Don't hide from me."

A different sort of pain filled Puck's expression, and I would've done anything to wash it away, to ease it by any means. My fingertips trailed over his cheeks, trying to bring comfort.

"I'm sorry," he rasped.

"You don't have to be sorry. You just need to let me in."

Puck let out a shuddered breath. "I keep thinking about how I've let you down. How I pushed you away at first. How I let you get taken. *Twice*. How I haven't protected you. And the threats are coming from all sides now. How the hell can I keep you safe?"

I stroked my fingers over his stubble. "Where is this coming from?" I knew we'd been facing a lot, but Puck had seemed good when I returned. Steady. His words now were filled with panic.

His jaw clenched, and the muscle there began pulsing wildly in a staccato beat I could feel beneath my fingertips.

"Puck, this is more than what happened recently. What's going on?" I pressed. I could feel it now, sheer panic raking against my emotional shields.

"My sister called."

I stilled. I remembered Puck telling me that he'd ceded leadership of his family's pack to his younger sister after his brother and his potential mate betrayed him. He'd told me it was too painful to be there after he was forced to end his brother's life. But I wasn't sure how much contact he still had with his sister and parents. Apparently, it wasn't much.

My hands trailed down Puck's neck to his chest, finally coming to a stop over his heart. "Is that okay? That she called?"

Puck's throat worked as he struggled to swallow. "I usually talk to them twice a year. Christmas and their birthdays."

An ache settled in my chest, sadness making itself at home there. "Why did she call now?"

"Remember how King put out the word that the Diablos had found their mate and threatened anyone who wanted to do her harm?"

I muttered a curse. That wasn't the way to find out that your brother or son had found their partner—through the black-market grapevine. "Was she mad?" I asked.

"I'm not sure if *mad* is the right word. But talking to her…it stirred things up. I started having nightmares from that time, and it heightened everything going on now. I feel like I'm jumping at every shadow."

Everything started to make sense. I leaned forward and nuzzled Puck's neck. "I'm right here. Not going anywhere. I'm safe and happy, just as long as you are."

His arms came around me, holding me to him. "I love you, Birdie. I don't know what I'd do without you."

"Good thing you'll never have to find out," I vowed.

"Clara, my sister, she wants to meet you."

I stiffened at that. "Meet me?" I squeaked.

Puck's chest began to shake with laughter. "Afraid of asshole MC members trying to kill her? Nope. Afraid of a wolf on a tear? Not at all. Afraid of meeting her mate's family? One hundred percent."

I nipped Puck's neck. "That's not nice."

Puck rolled me so I was on my back, and he was hovering over me in a position that had my legs hooking around his waist and heat flushing my skin. "I'm not sure now's the right time. I'm not sure I'm ready," Puck admitted. "I haven't seen her since I left."

That ache in my chest was back, deeper now. "I'd be with you. Maybe it's what you need. To finally face it."

Indecision warred on Puck's face before resolve set in. "Okay."

I grinned up at him. "Love you."

He lowered himself to me. "More than words."

And then he slid inside me. Puck's strokes began long and lazy as if he were in no rush at all. We soaked up every ounce of sensation and sentiment. And he showed me without words just how much he loved me.

CHAPTER TWENTY-EIGHT

Wren

THE BRUTAL CALL OF ONE OF THOSE PARTY AIR HORNS blasted into the soft glow of the rising sun. I jerked upright in bed, the guys all around me doing the same: Puck and Brix on my left, Locke and Kingston on my right, and Ender and Princess on the couch.

Princess hissed at the offender, and I had the urge to do the same.

"What the fuck?" Puck snarled.

"Time to train, Little Vixen," Rhys announced. "We've got lots of work to do."

"Someone kill him," Locke muttered, flopping back onto his pillow.

"I'm immortal," Rhys huffed.

Kingston narrowed his eyes on the vampire. "There are ways."

And there were. Lore said that an enchanted stake to the heart would do it. Or removing the vampire's head. Or burning them alive.

Rhys let out a little huff. "You could always try, but do you want the little firecracker to live or not?"

I threw off the covers, making the guys groan. "Nothing like the threat of death to get you going in the morning."

"I'll show him a threat of death," Brix growled as he rose from the bed and prowled toward Rhys.

The vampire simply tapped the side of his head. "Remember who gets the visions."

Brix kept right on moving. "If we remove his head from his body, think the visions will keep coming?"

"Possible," Ender said, stretching.

Princess leapt from the couch and stalked over to Rhys. She swiped at his calf and hissed before taking off down the hall.

"Ouch," Rhys said, bending down to rub his abused leg.

Puck grinned. "At least I'm not the only one she hates."

The windows to the gym were open, letting in the air that had tipped cooler with the arrival of early fall. I stretched toward one leg, grabbing my shoe.

"At least she's bendy," Rhys muttered.

"Stop staring at her cleavage," Puck griped, then smacked Rhys upside the head.

"Ow," Rhys said, affronted.

Puck simply arched an eyebrow.

Rhys straightened. "I can't ignore the fact that she's beautiful."

"I could pluck out your eyes," Brix offered. "That would help."

Locke snickered. "I'm so glad you haven't fully lost your edge."

Rhys's nose wrinkled as he warily looked at Brix. "I did think that whole feral-demon thing had eased."

"The psycho twins are still in full effect when they need to be," Puck assured him.

Kingston crossed his arms over his muscular chest. "Tell us what we're doing here."

"I told you," Rhys began. "Training. But we're waiting for one more."

"I'm here, I'm here," Hera grumbled. She half-stumbled into the gym, wearing pale-green sweats with different types of plants emblazoned on them. Her face was bare, and her strawberry-blond hair was tied up in a haphazard bun.

Rhys studied her. "Not a morning person?"

Hera bared her teeth at him. "You woke me up at five-thirty. In the *morning*."

"No rest for the wicked," Rhys said cheerily.

"Easy for you," Hera muttered. "Bloodsuckers don't sleep."

"You know," Rhys began, "I could start taking serious offense to that term."

"Maybe you'll remember that the next time you try to wake me up before dawn," Hera snarled.

Rhys held up both hands in surrender. "Touchy, touchy."

"Why do you need Hera here?" Locke asked. "No offense."

Hera waved him off. "None taken. I'd much rather be in bed."

"We're going to need her magic as the training progresses," Rhys explained. "But first, I wanted to go over some weaknesses I saw in Wren's hand-to-hand skills."

I bared my teeth at him. "What weaknesses?"

Rhys shifted into professional mode. "You drop your guard when you're thinking about your next attack move. It gives your opponent a chance to get in a blow."

I thought about the battle with Dent in the alleyway and cursed. The damn vamp was right. It had begun to slip twice, allowing a blow to find purchase. My back teeth ground together. "All right. What else?"

"Your speed is one of your greatest hand-to-hand skills, but you don't use it to its full potential," Rhys went on. "You're good with certain evasions, especially ducking low, but your footwork could be quicker. I'm going to set up some obstacle courses to help with that."

"Running, yay," I muttered.

Brix's lips twitched, and he bent to kiss my head. "I'll do them with you."

I looked up at him. "You're my favorite today."

"Hey," Puck protested. "I told you I'd make your favorite breakfast after training."

I grinned at him. "Maybe you'll be my favorite later."

"That's a little better," he huffed.

"I want to know what you need Hera for," Kingston demanded. "You aren't telling us something."

Rhys's focus moved to the Arcane alpha. "After hand-to-hand, we'll move to Wren's shifting speed. She needs to work on her quick changes."

I frowned. Rhys hadn't seen me shift, so how would he know if they were fast or slow?

"Why?" Kingston ground out.

Rhys was quiet for a moment, but then he spoke. "I had a vision. If we don't work on Wren's shifting and empath gifts, she'll die."

Each word detonated like a bomb, leaving shrapnel in its wake. It wasn't just the word *die* that left a heavy weight in the air, though. It was the word *empath*. No one but the guys knew what I was or that I had that gift. No one else knew because it put me at risk.

But, somehow, Rhys had found out. And as my mates all circled him, I knew this wouldn't go over well.

CHAPTER TWENTY-NINE

Kingston

I*F WE DON'T WORK ON WREN'S SHIFTING AND EMPATH GIFTS, she'll die."*

Rhys's words echoed in my head as the entire room crackled with energy. *Empath gifts.* Fear and rage battled for supremacy as I stalked forward. My hand lashed out, and I grabbed Rhys by the neck, lifting him into the air.

"Who told you?" I snarled.

Rhys clawed at my hand, his face turning an alarming shade of purple. "Told me what?"

"That she's an empath," I ground out as I gave him a good shake.

"Put him down, King," Ender called.

"Give me one good reason why."

Ender sighed. "He's playing right now. He could kick all our asses with one hand behind his back. He's going along for the moment, but that could change, and we need him."

I studied Rhys for a beat as he stopped clawing at me and simply let himself hang from my grip. Vampires were strong, but there was something else about Rhys. Something. . .*more.*

I released my hold on the bloodsucker and dropped him to the floor, but he landed easily. He cracked his neck as if loosening the muscles I'd abused. "No one told me anything. I saw it in a vision. That's all."

Hera shifted then, moving toward Wren, wonder in her eyes. "I knew there was something different about you." She reached out as if to touch my mate, and I moved in a flash.

Stepping between them, I bared my teeth at Hera. "You tell a single soul, and I will end you. You try to sell her out, and I'll make that end the most painful thing you can imagine."

My hold on my control was fraying. All I could think about were the mounting threats. So many things circling. So many possibilities for danger. But if word got out that Wren was an empath? What we currently faced would feel like nothing.

Hera rolled her eyes. "Relax, Alpha. I mean her no harm."

"And we're going to need her," Rhys said, still rubbing his neck. "The witch can help strengthen Wren's gift."

A different sort of energy crackled through the room. A second later, Rhys was flying through the air and landing in a heap against a pile of mats. Hera rubbed her fingers together. "Call me a witch again, and you'll find yourself struggling to breathe."

Rhys simply beamed up at her. "You know, I'm half in love with you."

"I told you," Hera ground out. "Not my type."

"It can be an unrequited love," Rhys said, leaning against the mats.

Hera let out a sound of disgust.

"Can we focus on what's important?" Locke broke into their standoff. "How can Hera make Wren's gift stronger?"

"I can't," Hera said, brushing herself off as if having her magic come into contact with Rhys had tainted it in some way.

I let out a low growl. "Someone explain."

Rhys stood and gestured to Hera. "My lady."

She snorted. "I can enchant herbs that will open Wren's mind."

That tidbit of information had Wren pushing to her feet. "Opening my mind just means I could get overloaded more quickly."

Five growls lit the air. None of us was particularly happy about that possibility.

Hera held up a hand. "Wait. When your mind is open, so is your gift. You will be hit with more emotion, but you will also be able to reach more deeply within yourself to deal with it."

Wren frowned as she mulled that over. "It could work."

"No," I clipped.

Wren bristled and sent me a scathing look. "Not your decision."

"I am the alpha of this pack," I shot back.

"And I'm not a member of this pack until Ender bites me, so I'm not under your rule."

"The little vixen has a point," Rhys singsonged as he glanced at Ender. "For once, your fear of commitment is coming through to help us."

"Fuck off. Like you're any better," Ender snarled.

A headache began to gather at my temples, the mounting pressure making itself at home there. And not for the first time in the past few months, I wanted to deck Ender.

Wren tugged her lip between her teeth, worrying the corner of it.

"What is it?" Hera asked gently.

Wren's gaze lifted to hers, and I saw so much uncertainty there. "I've spent my entire life trying to shove this gift down. I have layers upon layers of shields that my mother helped me create. I've only ever let myself open it in tiny slivers. I have no experience with letting it free."

My back teeth ground together. "Because it could kill you."

"Not helping," Brix warned.

"It is helping if it keeps her from getting dead. None of you are considering the fact that there's a reason empaths are practically extinct. Taking on too many negative emotions can drown them. And if she doesn't die, it could break her mind."

"Stop talking about me like I'm not here," Wren clipped.

I turned to face her, fear and rage springing to life yet again. "I love you with everything I have in me. I can't watch you put yourself in danger like this."

Something in Wren's demeanor softened. She moved into my space and lifted her hands to my cheeks. "Trust me to know my limits. Trust me to be strong enough to find a way."

"You're the strongest person I know," I rasped.

Wren stretched up onto her tiptoes and brushed her mouth against mine. "Then let me do this. Help me. We can figure it out together."

I hauled Wren into my arms, and she wrapped her legs around my waist as I touched my forehead to hers. "I love you, and this scares the hell out of me."

"It scares me, too. Which is why I need you with me."

"Okay," I breathed.

Wren pulled back a fraction so she could take in my face. "Really?"

I nodded and turned to face Rhys but kept Wren wrapped tightly in my arms. "What did you see in your vision? What does Wren need to be able to do?"

Rhys shook his head. "It's not like that. I get snapshots sometimes. A few seconds of moving pictures. But more than that, it's feelings. And the vision told me that Wren's empathy is the way through. That and her ability to shift."

I scowled, my frustration mounting. That wasn't exactly a lot to go on.

Wren seemed to sense my feelings because she cupped my cheek and gazed into my eyes. "It's a place to start."

I just hoped the path didn't end in death and destruction.

CHAPTER THIRTY

Wren

"IT SMELLS LIKE SOMETHING DIED," PUCK MUTTERED AS HE held his nose and walked closer to one of the gym's open windows.

He wasn't wrong. Whatever Hera was mixing in her ceremonial bowl smelled seriously rotten. But I couldn't keep myself from looking anyway.

Locke's curiosity had gotten the best of him, too. Hera scowled at him as he bent over the bowl to study the concoction. "Can I get some room?"

He grimaced. "Sorry. I just—what's in there?"

Hera's gaze flicked to me. "It's probably better if you don't know."

My hand went to my stomach as it did a series of flips. I wasn't sure if it was because of the possibilities of what I was about to consume, what I was about to face, or both.

I felt heat at my back, and the scent of mint and pine swirled around me. "You don't have to do this." Grit coated Kingston's words as he wrapped his arms around me from behind.

I leaned into his muscular chest. "Yes, I do."

A low, rumbling growl left his throat, and I felt the vibration in my back. "Little Warrior," he rasped.

"It'll be okay." I said the words, even if I didn't fully believe them. It was a promise to myself as much as anything.

Hera stopped mixing and closed her eyes. Her hands hovered over the ceremonial pot as she spoke some ancient words I didn't know. This wasn't caster magic. It was something else. I held my breath, waiting for sparks or a bang, something. But nothing happened.

Hera opened her eyes and lifted the bowl. "It's done."

"That's it?" Puck asked, voicing my thoughts.

Hera sent him a wan smile. "Magic isn't always showy."

"It's more fun when it is," Puck muttered.

Hera crossed to me and extended the small bowl. "You may want to hold your nose when you drink this. It'll go down easier."

I grimaced as I took in the greenish sludge. Before anyone could warn me off, I gulped it down and then almost threw up on the gym floor.

Bending over, I gagged but managed not to lose the contents of my stomach. Locke hurried over and helped me straighten. "Here, drink this. It'll cleanse the taste."

I chugged the pink drink he handed me. The taste of strawberries played over my tongue, washing away the worst of whatever I'd drunk before. I took a few steadying breaths. "Okay. I'm okay."

Brix looked at me with worried eyes. "How do you feel? Any different?"

I took stock of my body. I felt nothing but a faint tingling in my muscles, but that could've simply been from trying to keep from upchucking. Next, I took in my shields. I felt it then, an increase in pressure building against them.

Fear.

Hope.

Worry.

Anxiety.

There were more, but those were the overwhelming ones. The ones that pushed against me, demanding that I take them on, take them *in*.

"I feel…more," I whispered.

Hera smiled. "Good."

Rhys clapped his hands together. "Now, we can begin. First, we need someone for Wren to work on." He scanned the room, his gaze settling on Brix. "You. Your darkness will be a good challenge."

Brix instantly started shaking his head and backed up. "I can't. I can't cause her any more pain."

Rhys's mouth hardened into a thin line. "We need someone who will challenge her."

"Don't make him do it," I snapped at Rhys. I turned to Brix. "It's okay. You don't have to." I wasn't about to put him through more than he'd already gone through just because I needed a guinea pig.

"I'll do it." It was the voice I least expected. Deep, with an underlying hint of anger I hadn't picked up on before. Ender stepped forward, moving closer to me, something he rarely did. "I've got plenty of darkness for the little kitten to practice on."

I swallowed hard, my mouth suddenly feeling like cotton balls had been stuffed inside. My wolf howled her acceptance of this partner because she wanted to be closer to him. She wanted to mark, bite. *Claim.*

Rhys's lips twitched. "This is going to be so much fun."

A medicine ball hurtled toward Rhys's head. He turned, catching it at the last possible second, and scowled at Puck. "I'm trying to help."

"You're finding joy in Wren's struggles," he snarled. "You keep being an ass, and I'll keep throwing things at you. Next time, it'll be something sharper."

"Enough," Ender clipped. "Tell us what we need to do."

Rhys gave Puck one last glare before turning to me. "Wren, tell me how your gift usually works."

I had the sudden urge to bolt from the room. I was so used to hiding my gift from the world that sharing it felt like standing stark-naked in front of all of them and pointing out all my weaknesses. I forced myself to steel my spine and straighten my shoulders. We all started somewhere.

"I can feel heightened emotions from a distance, but I feel them strongest when I have skin-to-skin contact. It's easiest for me to heal that way, as well."

"All right. We'll start there," Rhys instructed. "And build in distance with time."

Ender's gaze locked on me as he moved closer. In three long strides, he was directly in front of me. The scents of cinnamon and cloves wove around me, pulling me in. My wolf pressed against my skin, wanting out, wanting the mate who hadn't claimed her yet.

That cotton-mouth feeling was back, and my hand trembled. Ender's gaze dropped to the offending appendage, and I swore I saw a hint of sympathy in his eyes. He moved slowly, threading his fingers through mine and squeezing.

An ache took root in my chest at the kindness. Along with it came a deep longing. Despite all the hurt he'd caused me along the way, every part of me wanted the final connection with Ender. I took a deep breath and tried to focus on the task at hand.

"When you're ready, Little Vixen, lower your shields," Rhys said.

The entire room held their breath as I stared at Ender. I looked into those swirling amber eyes and lowered my metaphysical shield, inch by inch. Inky black smoke rolled out and hit me hard, nearly making my knees buckle.

Ender instantly shot forward to steady me. His hand released mine but slipped beneath my hair, keeping the skin-to-skin contact. "Too much," he rasped. "A little at a time."

I breathed through the pain, the waves of agony that began as emotions and turned physical when they reached my body. I drew air in through my nose and let it out through my mouth, then closed my eyes and tried to unravel the knotted stew inside Ender.

One emotion flared strongest—one that had my eyes stinging and pressure building in my chest.

Self-hatred.

My eyes opened as I took in the man before me. He was so close I could almost taste a hint of cinnamon on my tongue. "I'm so sorry," I whispered.

Ender stiffened as fur rippled over his arms, his wolf wanting to be free. "Do it," he ground out.

I pulled on the thread, slowly taking it into me. But the pool of self-hatred was so deep it seemed never-ending. Sickness rolled through me, and sweat broke out on my brow as my legs began to shake more.

"That's enough," Kingston ordered.

"Not yet," Rhys snapped.

Ender's teeth elongated as he ran his nose along my neck. "Kitten," he growled.

My wolf howled, called by his. I wanted to bite, claim Ender as mine.

A second later, Ender ripped himself away from me, and I found myself falling. Brix was there to catch me, cradling me in his arms as light danced across my vision.

"I'm sorry," Ender croaked. "I can't."

A fresh wave of agony washed over me as Ender took off for the door. It felt as if a part of me were being ripped away.

Brix nuzzled my neck. "Breathe. Just focus on that. One breath at a time."

I struggled to refortify my walls as sweat gathered along my spine. I couldn't differentiate where the pain was coming from now. Was it my body or my soul? All I knew was that it hurt like hell.

"It's the bond," Hera said softly. "It wants completion. It's going to hound you until it has what it needs. You need to do it. It'll make you stronger."

My head snapped up, my vision swimming with the move. "I'll never bond for strength alone. I'd never steal that choice from Ender. He has to want it as much as I do."

I just worried that day may never come.

CHAPTER THIRTY-ONE

Locke

Wren's chest heaved as lines of pain mixed with the sweat on her brow. Her muscles twitched and quivered with fatigue. I bit the inside of my cheek to keep from suggesting she take a break. She'd nearly taken King's head off when he suggested it.

I'd thought switching from training her empath gifts to shifting would help, but this was almost worse to watch. Every time Wren's body contorted in her change, I felt the breaking of each bone. Each time she pushed her wolf to come on faster, I felt the twisting muscle and sinew.

Wren bent over, wrapping an arm around her ribs, trying to ease the pain. She wore the same clothing the young shifters going through their changes did. They were made of a specialty fabric with extra stretch and give. It allowed it not to tear each time they shifted, staying in place until their human forms returned.

Rhys frowned at her. "This should be much faster."

"Says the bloodsucker," Wren wheezed.

Hera let out a snicker.

Rhys glared at both of them and then turned to Puck. "When does your sister get here?"

Puck instantly bared his teeth. "I never told you I had a sister."

Rhys simply grinned and tapped the side of his head.

"That psychic thing freaks me out," Brix muttered.

"I think it's actually clairvoyance," King corrected.

Puck scrunched up his nose. "That means talking to dead people."

Wren rubbed her temples, pain streaking across her features. "None of this is helping."

Rhys studied her for a long moment. "I might be a vampire, but I've known plenty of shifters in my day, and you're slow."

I bit the inside of my cheek harder. I wanted to deck the damn vamp, but he was right. Wren *was* slower to bring on her shift than most wolves I knew. That didn't mean I could handle Rhys being so unkind.

I sent him a scathing look and moved across the space to Wren. Crouching low, I cupped her cheeks. "Hi."

Sadness and a hint of defeat swam in her turquoise eyes. "Hi."

"How do you feel?" I asked gently.

"Tired," she admitted.

I pulled her down to the mats and handed her a water bottle. She gulped the contents greedily, her brow furrowing. "What's in this? It tastes good."

"Electrolytes and vitamins. You need to replenish your energy."

She nodded and took another sip. When she set it down, she glanced around the room, looking embarrassed.

"Focus on me," I prodded. "It's just you and me."

Wren nodded, her eyes glistening.

"Hey," I whispered, stroking her cheeks. "What's going on?"

Those stunning turquoise depths filled. "I didn't get to spend much time in wolf form growing up. Bastian never wanted me to shift with the pack because I was submissive. So, when I did shift, it was alone. I'm not used to doing it around other people."

A low growl rumbled from my throat. It wasn't a sound my wolf typically made, but Bastian's treatment of Wren would get him there any time, especially around this particular issue.

"It's not your fault." I pressed my forehead to hers.

"Maybe not, but I still have to figure out a way around it. The truth is, I'm submissive, so shifting has always put me on edge. I had to watch my back doubly in wolf form because if I ran into others from our pack..."

Wren didn't have to finish the sentence for me to understand. Wolves wanting to prove their dominance would attack her without provocation. But it wasn't how packs *should* be. A truly healthy pack could appreciate each member for what they brought to the group. But I also knew what it was like to be thought of as less than simply because I wasn't dominant.

My thumbs stroked Wren's cheeks. "You and your wolf need to find a better balance. And she needs to know that she's safe with her new pack. Safe to be who she truly is."

Wren looked up at me, her eyes still glistening. "Sometimes, it feels like I'm too broken to ever trust that."

"Time," I whispered against her lips. "But we start with a pack run."

Ender made a sound from his spot in the corner, and we both looked at him. He cleared his throat and walked toward us, but his gaze was on Wren. "He's right. This'll be good. I just..."

Wren reached out and took his hand, squeezing it. "I know. Our wolves would bond, and it's not the right time."

Ender kept a hold of her hand and reached out with his other, stroking Wren's cheek. "My wolf would bite the shit out of you, Kitten."

A soft laugh escaped her lips, and relief swept through me. Ender might've had a freak-out yesterday, but he was trying, and that was what mattered. We all were.

"I'll see you after," she whispered.

Ender bent and brushed his lips over her hair. "See you." And then, he was gone.

I stood and offered a hand to Wren. "Ready?"

She nodded, but I could see the nerves humming below the surface.

"This will be really good," Kingston assured her. "For all of us."

Rhys's mouth curved. "Can I come?"

Kingston's expression immediately transformed into a scowl. "No."

"But I—"

"Save it, bloodsucker," Hera cut him off. "We can go find you a squirrel to snack on or whatever it is you eat."

Rhys's gaze narrowed on her. "Maybe I'll make an exception and snack on you."

Hera lifted her hand, sparks dancing between her fingers. "You can try..."

"Let's get out of here before they kill each other, and we have to clean up the mess," Puck muttered.

King, Brix, and Puck headed out the French doors with Wren and I following behind. Her footsteps slowed, and I looked down at her as I threaded my fingers through hers, assuring her that I'd be with her the whole way.

Wren looked up at me, worry swirling in those beautiful eyes. "What if I can't do this? What if I'm not strong enough to defeat my father?"

I gripped Wren's fingers tighter and brought my face closer to hers. "You are. Think of all you've made it through, all you've overcome. And now, you have us at your back, feeding you our unique strengths. Stronger together, remember?"

Wren's eyes shone in the early afternoon light. "Stronger together."

CHAPTER THIRTY-TWO

Wren

THE SUNLIGHT FILTERED THROUGH THE THICK TREES AS the guys began to undress. Normally, a glimpse of lean, defined muscles would've had my mind shifting to other places. Not today. Today, it was swirling with doubts and worries.

Locke's words echoed in my head. *"Stronger together."*

I wanted to believe in that, to trust that it would lead me through, but nerves still had a hold of me.

Puck stored his clothes and shoes in one of the hidey-holes in an old tree, then turned to walk toward me. He was completely comfortable in his nakedness, and my gaze roamed over his tan skin decorated by patches of ink I now knew Ender or Brix had put there. Puck didn't stop at a cautious distance, though; he moved straight into my space.

His hand skated across my jaw. "This will be fun. Just like you taking me down the other day. Your wolf had no problem calling on her dominance then."

Something eased inside me because he was right. My wolf had only been thinking of one thing: bringing her mate back to her. "I think I need to get out of my head and out of my own way."

Puck's hands dropped to the hem of my workout tank. "I can help with that." He slowly tugged the shirt up and over my head, the built-in bra going with it. He folded it carefully and handed it to Brix, who stowed it in the tree.

Then Puck dropped to his knees, looking up at me with reverence. He lifted one leg and removed my sneaker, then the other. His eyes locked on mine as he hooked his fingers in the band of my workout pants and slowly tugged them down.

I could've shifted with clothes on since I was wearing the specialty gear, but my wolf wouldn't have been as free. She wouldn't have been able to get that fur-to-fur contact or feel completely at ease. But now that I was gazing down at Puck, completely bare to him as he carefully folded my pants, I felt exposed.

Only it wasn't in a bad way. And as I looked around the small clearing, my soul let out a sigh. We were all exposed, vulnerable to one another, but safe in doing so because of the bond we shared. Tears pricked my eyes for a whole new reason. Because I shared the ultimate bond with these incredible men.

Puck pushed to his feet and kissed me so softly it made my heart ache. "Ready to fly, Birdie?"

"I'm ready," I whispered.

He stepped back, and Kingston stepped in. He let out a low, rumbling sound, almost like a purr, a call from his wolf to mine. "I'm assuring her that I'll be here waiting."

That made the ache intensify but in the best way. "Okay," I whispered.

Slowly, the men around me shifted. Brix changed to his hauntingly beautiful, jet-black counterpart. Puck called on his golden god. Locke brought forth his hypnotizing, reddish-brown half. And King presented his silver-gray, almost magical beast.

They were all stunning, and they were all mine. Just seeing

them that way had my wolf launching to the surface. She came on faster this time, still not quite as quick as my mates but better than I'd managed to achieve all day.

But it was more. The shift felt as easy as breathing. No pain. Only sweet relief at being free.

I shook out my fur as I stood on four paws.

Puck padded up to me and licked the side of my muzzle. I returned the favor, wanting him to carry my scent markers, too.

Brix nipped my shoulder like only the master of pleasure and pain would. I turned and quickly bit his hindquarter, and he let out a playful growl.

Locke brushed against me, his whole body greeting mine with the sweetest embrace. I let out a sound of pure pleasure at the contact.

Kingston tipped his head back and let out an alpha howl. The sound shot through the air and sent vibrations through everything it encountered—even me. The feeling was like thousands of King's fingers brushing through my fur at once.

He lowered his head, then circled me and nudged my side as if to say, "*Let's go.*" And we did.

We raced through the stream and into the mountains. We ran up trails in a game of tag before racing back down again. There were no battles for dominance or need to prove one's strength. There was simply fun and togetherness.

It was so unlike my father's pack. So much more like a true family. One born of choosing one another instead of the link blood could force on you. And knowing that I got to choose these men over and over again for the rest of my days was the best gift I could imagine.

We all slowed to a walk as we reached the clearing where we'd stashed our clothes, but not before taking a dip in the creek to wash off the effects of the run. The cold water felt like heaven on my fur.

One by one, we shifted back, and that came easier for me now, too. My bones cracked and reformed into my human half, and I stretched, working out the kinks.

Puck tossed me my clothes and then grabbed his, but stilled as he looked down at the phone in his hand, his expression unreadable.

"What is it?" I asked, instantly moving to his side.

His throat worked as he swallowed. "My sister. She's here."

CHAPTER THIRTY-THREE

Puck

ALL THE PEACE I'D GAINED FROM OUR PACK RUN VANISHED in a second at the text on the screen.

Clara: *I'm here. Unlock this ridiculous gate.*

The text was so Clara. The fact that our family was considered royalty on the other side of the world had given her an affinity for history. She wouldn't care for the modern style of our gates or house.

Me: *I'm surprised you even figured out how to text.*

Clara answered with two middle finger emojis, and I barked out a laugh.

"That's good, right?" Wren asked tentatively as she pulled on her clothes.

I quickly donned mine, a fresh wave of nerves hitting me. "It's just...it's been so long."

I avoided the guys' stares, too ashamed of the fact that it had been such a long time since I'd seen my family in person.

Kingston squeezed my shoulder. "You're seeing her now. That's what matters."

"And she came all this way," Wren went on. "That means she loves you."

I wanted both of them to be right, but I was still so unsure.

Brix shot me a grin. "You know one thing. You're only going to piss off the queen if you leave her out there waiting."

I cursed because he was right. We all took off at a jog for the house, and that wasn't a bad thing. My muscles were wound impossibly tight from the epic run we'd just had. But as the house came into view, anxiety flared again.

Wren slid her hand through mine. "I'm with you. Whatever comes our way."

I looked down at her, feeling those words carve themselves into my heart. "Whatever comes our way," I echoed.

Locke held the back door for us, and we all filed into the house, but I didn't let go of Wren's hand. My shifter hearing picked up the sound of a door slamming out front.

"I let them in," Rhys called from the entryway.

"This isn't your goddamned house," King bellowed.

Rhys let out a huff. "That's not exactly the way to make someone feel welcome."

"Good," King shot back.

I didn't have it in me to banter with them now. My mouth had gone dry, and my pulse thrummed in my neck.

Kingston moved to the door since it was his role as Alpha to greet any guests, especially the leader of another pack. He opened it and stepped back, welcoming my sister and the four guards surrounding her.

My breath caught in my throat at the sight of Clara. She looked exactly the same and yet completely different. Long, blond hair hung in loose waves around her, and her green eyes shone like glittering emeralds. She was dressed smartly in billowing silk pants and a soft cashmere sweater, rings glinting on her fingers. She looked so damn grown up now it had pressure mounting on my chest.

"Welcome to Crescent Creek and the Arcane pack," Kingston greeted smoothly.

Clara inclined her head ever so slightly to King, a show of deference to his alpha status here. "Thank you for having me. These are my personal guards." She stepped aside to reveal the four shifters behind her, two women and two men, all of various ages.

"Mei." An Asian woman stepped forward with a slight bow, but I didn't miss the daggers at her hips.

"Archie." An older, redheaded man with some silver at his temples ducked his head in the barest dip.

"Henry." A younger man with dark hair inclined his head in a more appropriate acknowledgment.

"Eliza." A red-haired woman with curves for days gave a half curtsey, half bow.

"You're all welcome," Kingston greeted, ushering them in.

Clara's eyes locked with mine, and she lost all sense of propriety. A huge grin split her face, and then she was running. I dropped Wren's hand just as Clara launched herself at me. She hit me full force, startling a laugh out of me. I swung her around. "Fucking hell, I missed you, Clare Bear."

She let out a sniff. "I missed you too, Pucker."

I chuckled, letting her down. "I didn't miss that nickname."

Clara just grinned through watery eyes. "Gonna be using it as much as I can." She turned, taking in Wren, her eyes warming even more. "You must be Wren."

Wren returned my sister's smile, holding out a hand. "It's wonderful to meet you."

Clara bypassed the handshake and went in for a hug. "I'm so happy he found you."

Wren's gaze met mine as she embraced my sister, her eyes going misty. "I'm so happy you're here."

Clara released Wren, her gaze doing a sweep. "How'd you land her, Pucker? She's obviously way out of your league."

I let out a scoff as the rest of my pack laughed. "Little sisters."

Clara's eyes twinkled. "You missed me like crazy."

I squeezed her shoulder. "More than you'll ever know."

The fire crackled as Clara sipped her tea, and Wren curled into me, her soft breaths of sleep wafting over my chest in a steady, reassuring beat. The rest of the guys had gone to bed, along with Clara's guards, Rhys, and Hera. We were finally truly alone.

Clara set her teacup on the saucer she had perched on the side table. "You've built a beautiful life here for yourself." Her nose wrinkled. "Even if you do let vampires in your midst."

I chuckled, shifting Wren so I could take a sip of my tea. It felt like a little piece of home, having tea with my little sister. "Trust me, having a vampire in our midst wouldn't be my first choice, but he's proven…helpful in the past."

It wasn't just Ender that Rhys had helped out. It was our whole pack. And despite his questionable tactics, I knew he had some unique insights.

Clara's lips twitched. "I can't wait to hear more about that."

"What about you?" I prodded. "How's life at home? Are you happy?"

A wistful smile stretched across her face. "I love it there. Love leading our pack. But I can admit, I'm longing for a mate of my own."

I reached out and squeezed her hand. "They'll come. Maybe when you least expect it."

"Maybe," Clara said softly.

I swallowed hard. "And Mum and Dad? How are they? Really."

"Good. Healthy, even as they're getting older, but they miss you."

A pang lit along my sternum. "I just…I haven't been ready to face them. To face home."

"Puck, what happened wasn't your fault. It's all on Theo and Alice. I just wish I could've challenged her then, too," Clara spat.

I shook my head. "We didn't need more death."

"Maybe not, but I hate that I've been without my brother all these years because of her."

The pang transformed into an ache and settled deep in my bones. "I'm sorry, Clare Bear. I needed to get my head on straight."

"And now? Is it straight?" she pressed.

"It's getting there. Wren…she's changed things for me."

Clara's expression softened. "I can see that. And I'll be forever grateful."

"Me, too."

As if half-roused by her name, Wren mumbled something in her sleep and burrowed deeper into me. My lips twitched, and I shifted to pull her fully into my arms. "I'm going to carry her to bed. I'll be back."

"All right," Clara whispered. She watched me as I lifted Wren, a gentleness in her expression. "Puck?"

"Hmm?" I asked, pausing before heading down the hall.

"Please don't let us go this long without being together again."

I could feel her pain then, like a living, breathing thing. It hurt and was a gift all at once. "We won't. I promise."

CHAPTER THIRTY-FOUR

Wren

I TWISTED IN THE SHEETS IN A BATTLE BETWEEN WAKING AND sleeping, something pushing at me. A need, I realized. *Blood.* I craved it. Needed to feel it spilling out over my hands, warm and thick and mine.

I blinked against the darkness of the room, the only glow that of the small night-lights the guys had put in all over the house to make sure I was never alone in the dark. Only it didn't scare me like it used to. It didn't have the same haunting effect it once did. Maybe because, for the first time in my life, I felt safe. Because I was never alone in the dark.

My eyes slowly assimilated to the low light all around me until I could make out Locke on one side of me and Brix on the other. My heartbeat stuttered in my chest as I took in Ender on the couch, a blanket pulled over him.

The last thing I remembered was talking with Puck and Clara on the sofa. I knew I must've fallen asleep, and someone had likely carried me to bed. I glanced at the bedside clock. It read 3:33 in the morning. I thought of making a wish, but then that weird urge hit me again.

Blood. All of it. Spilling out onto my hands, power coming into me.

I shook my head, trying to clear the pain pulsing there. It wasn't like the emotions I normally felt. It was more. These were thoughts.

I moved from the bed without thinking—the urge to search out the source was too strong not to. I stilled at the foot of the bed, looking at the men in the room. I could've woken one, but the thought of trying to explain what I was experiencing stopped me. Still, I paused by the dresser and pulled out the knife that had become my safety blanket.

Slipping from the room, I moved to the top of the stairs and stilled. I tried to picture where everyone was staying. The four guards down and to the left, along with Clara. Puck and Kingston, likely in their rooms, down and to the right. Rhys and Hera on the first floor and to the right.

I closed my eyes and searched for the feelings, the thoughts. The ache in my head intensified. To the right. I could feel it. Almost like a glowing beacon.

My stomach twisted, and a sick feeling made a home there. *Rhys.* He might not drink human blood, but that didn't mean he didn't crave it. Maybe I was feeling his dream.

I slipped down the stairs to the second floor and stilled again, searching. The feeling didn't seem like it was coming from the lower floor; it felt as though it were coming from this one. My feet were already moving, telling me something my brain didn't yet understand.

I moved to the right toward Kingston's and Puck's bedrooms, stopping between them as I tried to pin down the exact location. But I didn't need my gift; I only needed my eyes. The door to Puck's room was slightly ajar.

Everything in me stilled as my hold on the blade tightened.

I flipped it open on instinct, moving toward the open door. The moment I slipped inside, my blood ran cold.

Puck lay sprawled in the bed like a starfish, mouth slightly open and breathing so deeply I knew he was oblivious to everything. But a figure stalked toward him, broad and shadowed, a knife clenched in their hand.

"I wouldn't do that if I were you," I growled.

The figure whirled, the moonlight hitting his face and illuminating red hair and a beard. Shock swept through me at the sight of Archie, one of Clara's guards. His face twisted with sheer hatred. "You think some submissive mate of Clara's worthless brother is going to stop me?"

I moved into a fighting stance. "Oh, I'll do more than stop you. I'll make you wish you were never born."

Archie scoffed. "Please. Puck is a waste of space. His brother would've been the ultimate alpha if Puck wouldn't have gotten in his way. But Clara is worthy, at least. And I won't have Puck deciding he wants to reclaim the throne."

Anger surged at the guard's moronic reasoning. Puck wanted nothing to do with the throne or his old pack. And he was clearly the more dominant wolf, given the fact that he'd defeated his brother all those years ago. But, sometimes, there was no reasoning with blind loyalty.

Archie charged, counting on his size and speed to win. But I was quicker. I lifted my blade and hurled it at him. Shock widened Archie's eyes, but his reaction time was too slow. The blade struck true, right in the guard's left eye.

He let out a choked sound for a single second and then collapsed to the floor in a heap. It was then that I realized the bloodlust was gone. Snuffed out with Archie.

Then a deep voice sounded from behind me. "Not bad, Kitten."

CHAPTER THIRTY-FIVE

Wren

The lights in the room flicked on as Ender surveyed the damage. "That's not going to come out of the rug anytime soon."

"What the hell is going on?" Kingston hissed, striding in from across the hall. His eyes flared and flashed silver as he took in the body on the floor. "What. Happened?"

I looked from the body to Puck, a little panic seeping in. He hadn't woken, not even slightly. But his chest rose and fell steadily; he even let out the occasional snore.

"I-I felt something," I stammered as anxiety pressed down on me.

Ender crossed the room in three long strides, then slid his hand beneath my hair to squeeze my neck. "Just breathe, Kitten. No one's mad at you. You can kill anyone you damn well please."

"Ender," King rebuked. "Not helpful."

"She can, and you know she had a reason."

"I'm just trying to discern what that is," King argued.

"I felt bloodlust," I cut in.

They both stilled.

"It was different, though. I could feel his thoughts. Knew some of them," I went on.

"It's because they were darker," a new voice said. We all turned to see Rhys strolling into the room, looking like he'd been working out. But I guessed if you didn't sleep, you had to fill your evenings somehow. His eyes narrowed on the fallen form, his mouth twisting in disgust. "Your mind is more open, Little Vixen. You'll pick up on things you couldn't before."

I shuddered, and Ender pulled me against him. The move was so unusual for him that it only made my head spin more. But that didn't stop me from soaking up his warmth.

"Tell us what happened," Kingston said softly.

"Like I said, I sensed bloodlust. I followed the feeling, and it led me to right outside Puck's room. The door was open, so I came in. I saw a figure with a knife. When they turned, I recognized Archie. He started talking about how Puck's brother was the rightful alpha and that he couldn't risk Puck returning to their pack."

"Bloody idiot," Clara snarled, striding into the room, her other guards on her heels, Brix and Locke moving behind them. "*Traitorous* idiot," she amended. She moved to the body and spat on it.

"Whaaaas going on?" Puck slurred, finally starting to come around.

Kingston's brow furrowed. "He sounds drugged."

Hera entered the room and crossed to the bed. Her hands hovered over Puck as she closed her eyes. "He is. Some sort of sleep aid. Give me a moment."

As Hera began chanting, Brix and Locke moved to me. Locke looked worried, while Brix had more of a pissed-off bent to his expression. Locke cupped my face. "You're all right?"

I nodded against his hold. "I'm fine. Promise." I scowled at the body. "I would like my knife back, though."

Kingston arched a brow. "Don't you mean *my* knife?"

I lifted my chin. "I've grown partial to it. It's gotten me out of a few jams now."

Kingston moved to kiss me quickly. "It's yours."

"I'll make sure you get it back," Clara assured me.

"You don't know what happened here," the guard named Eliza argued. "They could've lured Archie into a trap."

Clara snorted. "In my brother's bedroom? At almost four in the morning?"

Mei scowled at the body. "He wasn't happy about coming here."

"No, he wasn't," Henry agreed.

Hera's chanting stopped, and the room went quiet. Puck blinked a few times, and his hand went to his head. "Jesus, Clare Bear. Did we do shots or something?"

Clara's mouth twisted in a wry smile that quickly dropped away. "No. I'm guessing Archie slipped something into your tea when he brought it to us before he retired for the evening. How do you feel?"

Puck sat up fully, looking from his sister to the man on the floor. "Doing better than he is."

Locke strode toward the body, studying it before sliding a phone out of the man's jacket pocket. He glanced at Clara. "May I?"

"This man just tried to kill your bondmate and my brother. You can take his head if you need it."

"That's more Brix's territory," Ender muttered.

Brix simply flipped him off, but Locke's fingers were already flying over the device's screen.

Puck scanned the room. "What the hell happened?"

"Archie boy tried to off your ass, but Wren saved your life," Ender explained helpfully.

Puck's gaze flew to me. "Are you okay? He didn't hurt you, did he?"

"I'm fine. He never got close to me," I assured him.

"Your mate has some serious knife skills," Clara said, admiration clear in her voice.

Puck rose from the bed, slightly unsteady at first, but it didn't take him long to reach me. He pulled me into his arms and breathed deeply. "Love you, Birdie. And not just because you saved my ass."

My hands fisted in his tee. "I love you, too. Don't scare me like that again."

"I'll do my best not to get on the short list of some maniac's revenge plot again."

"Good," I huffed.

Puck kissed me, long and slow.

"Gross," Clara muttered. "I do *not* need to see that."

Puck sent her a scathing look. "Then turn away."

"Guys," Locke interjected. "I'm in."

We all turned to face him as he tapped on the screen, then seemed to scroll. Locke's typically easy-going demeanor changed in an instant. His expression went thunderous.

"What?" King demanded.

Locke looked up slowly, his gaze moving not to Kingston but to me. "Archie was in contact with Bastian. He wanted to know what the reward would be if he killed the entire Arcane pack and delivered Wren back to him."

CHAPTER THIRTY-SIX

Wren

ANGRY ENERGY CRACKLED THROUGH THE AIR. IT SWIRLED and pulsed, making a home in all of us for one reason or another. But a sense of true dread settled in my bones. Because even with King's warning to all supernaturals, there would always be beings willing to team up with Bastian for one reason or another. None of this would end until Bastian himself was ended.

Clara muttered a series of admirable curses as she turned to the rest of her guards. "Your phones. Now. And I'll give you one chance to come clean. Tell me if you were in on this, and I'll make your deaths merciful. If you don't, and I find out that you were a part of this, I will torture you for months on end before I kill you."

A grin spread slowly across Rhys's face as he turned to Puck. "I like your sister."

Puck glared at the vampire. "Stay the hell away from her."

Clara gave him a head-to-toe sweep. "Under different circumstances, I might dip a toe in that pool."

Puck gagged.

She flipped him off, but the amusement slipped from Clara's face as she turned back to her guards. "Phones. Now."

All three instantly turned over their devices. Clara collected them and handed them to Locke. "Feel free to search all our belongings, as well. My personal phone is on my nightstand."

King's brows rose. "You'd let us search yours, too?"

"You're my brother's pack. Your trust is important to me." Clara cracked her neck. "Now, I really need to spar. Who's in?"

"Me," I said quickly. "I need to hit something."

By the time the body had been cleared from Puck's room and we'd all made it down to the gym, the sun was rising and sending beautiful pink rays through the forest. I rolled my shoulders, testing the tension that had made its home there. It wasn't insignificant.

Even though Clara's phone as well as her guards' had been free of any communications with Bastian, the weight of the night's events still felt heavy for all of us. A traitor had found their way onto our territory. Worse, they'd been invited in.

"I'm not sure this is such a good idea," Kingston said quietly. "You've been through more than your fair share lately, and your head may not be in the right place for sparring."

"King—"

"He has a point," Rhys cut in.

"Says the man willing to let me get jumped in the name of training," I spat.

Rhys held up both hands. "Touchy, touchy. I was just thinking this might be good timing for Clara to help you with your shift."

Clara's brow furrowed. "What's going on with your shift?"

"Noth—"

"It's slow," Rhys said, cutting me off.

I sent the vampire a look that should've had his balls climbing back up into his body. "Remember that knife in the eye from a couple of hours ago?"

Rhys just grinned. "Love your violent streak. Channel that with the shifting business."

I pulled the knife from my pocket, opened it, and hurled it in Rhys's direction. It just barely nicked his ear before coming to rest in the far wall.

Rhys clutched the side of his head. "That was uncalled for, Little Vixen."

"That was *exactly* called for," Clara argued. "The shifting process is incredibly personal, and you should never insult a shifter's relationship with their animal that way."

Pressure built behind my eyes, and my wolf let out a hum of satisfaction at Clara's words. She rather liked Puck's sister.

Clara moved toward me, hooking her arm in mine. "Carry on, the lot of you. Wren and I have some business to attend to."

"What about me?" Puck asked.

"You, too, Pucker."

He made a face.

"Don't pout. It's not attractive, and Wren is already too good for you," Clara said, leading me toward the back doors.

Brix choked on a laugh, and Puck turned to him. "You and me, hand-to-hand."

"That's not going to end well," I mumbled.

"It never does. The male ego is a fragile thing."

A laugh bubbled out of me as I let Clara lead me farther into the trees.

"There's something many alphas miss," Clara began. "Submission is the ultimate power." She released her hold on me. "Alphas only hold the cards because *you* let them. You can revoke it at any time. It is a choice. Always. And your tender, caretaking spirit is something all of us alphas yearn for, even if we don't admit it."

I studied Clara for a long moment. With her blond hair swept back in a ponytail and her face free of makeup, she looked younger. I couldn't believe that she had so much on her shoulders already. "I know, I think you might hold some of those gifts."

Clara's mouth curved. "Caretaking, even now. You don't want me to feel down about myself."

My lips twitched. "Maybe so, but it doesn't make it any less true."

"Perhaps. But for now, let's work on harnessing your unique power. Do you feel comfortable shifting in front of me?"

Nerves hit me fast and hard, but I nodded.

"All right. Let me get a look at the process."

I swallowed and stripped down, leaving my clothes in a pile. Clara's focus remained on my face, the way most shifters did. We were used to getting naked in front of one another, but that wasn't an excuse to stare.

I tried to remember how it had felt to be with the guys when they shifted, the peace that had found me there. I called on my wolf, asking her to come, inviting her to find that peace with me again. It was faster than it had been with Rhys but still clunky in places.

As I found myself on four paws, Clara crouched, offering me a hand to sniff. "I want your wolf to trust me, too. It'll be easier that way."

I sniffed her hand, picking up undertones in her scent that reminded me of Puck. That had me licking her palm in an offer of friendship. Clara laughed, the sound light. "Good. Now, shift back."

I did as she asked, finding myself on two feet again. "It's better than it was, but it's still awkward."

Clara nodded. "You've protected your wolf for so long. You need to let her protect you, as well."

I mulled that over. I had. I never fought in wolf form if I could avoid it, and it would hurt if someone doubted my human half that way.

"Trust. Don't force," Clara went on. "Don't push the shift. Just let it come. Allow your wolf to lead. The more you two are one, the stronger *all* your gifts will be."

I nodded. This time, I closed my eyes and simply breathed. I listened to the wind in the trees and the sound of my heartbeat. Then, I welcomed my wolf in. I let her decide when the shift should happen.

Her answer? Instantaneously.

Faster than I'd ever felt before, the crack of bones shifted me to four paws once again. Clara hooted with joy and jumped in the air.

"Was I right, or was I right?" Rhys called through the trees.

"Stop creeping on Wren when she's shifting," Brix snarled.

Kingston let out a low growl. "Why hasn't someone killed him yet?"

One corner of Clara's mouth tugged up. "I think Wren could give that a stab in her wolfy form."

My wolf pounced. All in good fun, of course.

CHAPTER THIRTY-SEVEN

Wren

"I have a bruise on my ass, you know," Rhys grumped. "Sitting on this stool is painful."

I poured him some whiskey from behind the bar at Arcane and rolled my eyes. "Do vampires even bruise?"

Rhys huffed out a breath. "No. But if we did, I'd have one. That was completely uncalled for."

"Oh, it was completely called for," Clara argued.

"Damn straight," Puck said, lifting a glass to his sister.

Clara clinked her shot glass to his and tipped it back.

"Three against one," I singsonged to Rhys.

"Rude," he mumbled, taking a long drink of whiskey.

I leaned against the back bar. "So, you like human food and drinks?"

"Human food tastes like cardboard, but I *love* alcohol." The adoring way Rhys looked at his glass said exactly that.

"Why do you eat, then?" I pressed.

Rhys straightened, tension weaving its way through his shoulders. "Long story."

"A no-go zone," Clara surmised.

Puck studied the vampire for a long moment. "You know, it seems quite unfair that you seem to know all our secrets, and we know none of yours."

Rhys grinned, the charmer mask back in place. "Exactly how I like it."

But I'd gotten a glimpse beneath the mask, and there was a bone-deep sadness there. Loneliness.

"Come on," Rhys said, sliding off his stool. "It's time to head to the gym."

I glanced at the clock on the wall and saw that it was five past the end of my and Puck's shift. "Dina, do you need us to stay?" I called.

She waved us off. "I'm good until the dinner shift gets here. I've got my trusty bat if anyone causes trouble."

Clara beamed. "I *love* her."

"That's because you have fabulous taste," I said, setting my order pad on one of the shelves behind the bar.

The moment the four of us headed for the door, Clara's guards silently surrounded her.

"Doesn't that get old?" Rhys asked.

"Not when I'm partial to breathing," Clara shot back.

The remark had Puck's brow furrowing, and I understood why. I couldn't help wondering what sorts of threats Clara had faced to make a security detail necessary.

She quickly changed the subject as we walked across the parking lot to Crescent Kingdom. "I like seeing this side of the human world. Our pack lands are so removed from the humans that we don't get the same slice of life. Pucker, your bar is charming."

Puck let out a snort. "Brace yourself for the human contingent we're about to meet."

I rolled my lips over my teeth, trying to keep from laughing. "I can't wait to watch you kick their asses."

Clara let out a low laugh. "It is fun to put men in their place, isn't it, Wren?"

Rhys rubbed his backside. "My ass is still complaining about the last show of force from you two. Simmer down."

I didn't hold in my laugh this time.

Henry stepped forward, holding the door for the rest of us, but it was Mei and Eliza who took the lead, scanning the space for any intruders. The moment all of us stepped inside, the sparring and heavy bag work slowed or stopped altogether as everyone stared.

"Now, this place I *love*," Clara said almost reverently.

"Thanks," Kingston said with a twitch of his lips as he walked up. "Welcome to Crescent Kingdom. It's an MMA gym, but we get some who tend more toward boxing."

Clara scanned the room. "It's a great space."

Juan moved toward us from where he'd been working out on a heavy bag. "Who is this absolute *goddess*, and why have we never met?"

He took Clara's hand and lifted it to his lips. In turn, she let out an honest-to-goodness giggle.

"Oh, hell no," Puck muttered. "Stay the fuck away from my sister. Everyone."

Juan's eyes widened, but he didn't let go of Clara. "Wait," he whispered. "Do you go wolfy, too?"

She spun on Puck. "You told the humans?"

He winced. "We didn't really have a choice."

"We thought they were aliens for a while," Juan explained without worry.

"Gods," Clara swore.

I squeezed her shoulder. "They're trustworthy."

"I hope you're right."

"Can I show you around?" Juan offered to Clara.

"No, you fucking can't," Puck clipped.

It was the wrong thing to say because Clara simply slid her arm through Juan's and batted her eyelashes at him. "I'd love that."

Brix sauntered up and clapped Puck on the shoulder. "Rookie move."

"Oh, piss off," Puck shot back and strode toward the treadmills, glaring at Juan the whole way.

Brix burst out laughing but moved into my space and brushed his lips against mine. "Missed you."

"I missed you, too. Want to spar after I warm up?" I asked.

"Hell, yeah, I do. We'll have to make do with one of the fight mats, though. Clyde's using the ring for a lesson."

I looked over to see Clyde working with a man who was vaguely familiar as Franco and Ender looked on from opposite sides of the ring. "No problem."

King dropped a kiss on my temple. "Make sure your muscles are nice and loose. You've had a lot of training these past few days."

"Sir, yes, sir." My lips twitched as I saluted him.

"Little Warrior, I like the sound of that a little too much."

My belly heated. "Don't distract me."

King grinned. "I'd never."

I made a *pssh* sound but headed for the jump ropes. Before long, I was warmed up and circling Brix on a fight mat. We wore mouthguards and fight gloves, but I knew neither of us would take it too far.

We traded punches and kicks without any serious heat, but when I saw an opening, I struck out with a sweep, taking Brix to the mat. He landed with a thud as our onlookers let out a series of cheers. I straddled him and pinned his arms, but Brix let me.

I shook my head. "You could've tried a little harder."

"Maybe I wanted to be pinned by you," he growled low.

I kissed him quickly and leapt to my feet. I offered him

a hand up, but a roar of fury had me spinning around. A figure charged toward me. Someone I knew. But also. . .not.

There were only two things I saw as Franco ran at me. His eyes had gone completely black, and he had one of the largest daggers I'd ever seen.

CHAPTER THIRTY-EIGHT

Wren

Everything happened so fast it was like I could only pluck individual snapshots out of the air. Those haunting, dead eyes. The glint of the blade in the air. The pure fury in Franco's expression.

And then something else—something that had everything in me seizing in sheer panic. A flash of movement I recognized instantly as Ender. Movement that put him directly in Franco's path at the last possible second.

The knife struck Ender in the chest, just beneath his shoulder, and he let out a grunt of pain as he sent Franco stumbling back in pain. A second later, Brix sent two knives flying at the man. They pinned him to the wall as he spat and struggled, raging in a language I'd never heard before.

The entire gym erupted, but I only had eyes for Ender. Only the handle of the knife was visible now. It was bejeweled with ancient language on the handle. And the etchings were glowing.

I could hear Clyde in the background, trying to calm the patrons, telling them to stay put. All of that was minimized by the fact that Franco was hissing and spitting like some sort of zombie.

"I'll handle the humans," Eliza clipped. For a brief second, I feared that her *handling* them meant slaughtering them all where they stood, but as I glanced over my shoulder, I saw her eyes sparking with golden fire.

She made eye contact with each human other than Clyde and Juan, holding them captive with that stare as she spoke an incantation and then wove a different sort of story. "You came to the gym and had a normal workout. You had to leave early because a pipe burst. You won't return until tomorrow."

They all went to grab their belongings and filed out of the gym, calm as can be.

"How the hell?" Clyde muttered.

I didn't care how, just that Eliza had done it. I turned back to Ender and moved in closer, but he held out a hand to stop me. "Don't. I need to—" Ender gripped the handle and pulled the blade from his chest, letting out a pained groan and then a curse.

As the knife clattered to the floor, Franco writhed and fought harder, as though he'd do anything to get to that blade. Ender bent over, his chest heaving. "Fucking hell."

I couldn't stay back any longer. My hand went to his shoulder, trying to help him straighten. "Let me see."

"Are we going to talk about the fact that my best friend looks like the fucking walking dead?" Juan snapped. "What the hell is happening? It's like he's possessed."

Clara moved toward Franco, showing no fear as she studied him. "Not possessed. Spelled."

"What in the actual fuck?" Juan cried.

Kingston shoved his phone back into his pocket. "Hera's on her way." He turned to Puck's sister. "What do you know?"

I helped Ender stand fully, Brix at my side. And then true panic hit me. The wound. It was deep and oozing blood. But the blood bubbled as it spilled from him. "It's not healing," I croaked. "Why isn't it healing?"

Clara turned, her focus dropping to the blade on the mat. It no longer glowed, but the jewels in the handle still glittered under the gym's bright lights. "It's an enchanted blade. It's meant to capture someone's soul essence, along with their power. But it only works if it's stabbed into the heart."

My hand instantly went to Ender's wound, trying to discern how deep it had gone and exactly where it had landed. Panic swept through me in a vicious blaze. "It didn't get your heart, did it?"

Sweat broke out on Ender's brow. "Kitten, my soul's right where it should be. It's all good."

But the pallor of his skin said otherwise. He was pale and clammy as he stumbled slightly. Brix caught him. "We need to lay him down."

"I'm fine," Ender bit out.

"You're not," Brix snapped. "Now, lie down and shut up."

"I'd like it a lot better if Kitten was ordering me around," he mumbled, wincing as Brix got him on the floor.

I sank to the mat next to him and took his hand. "Why?"

"I'm getting kind of partial to you, Kitten," Ender wheezed.

Clara moved in closer, glancing at Brix. "Put pressure on the wound until your healer gets here. She'll know what to do."

Brix instantly did as she asked, leaning his full weight on Ender's chest. Ender let out a stream of curses. "You might want to lay off the cookies."

More sweat streamed from his face, and I gripped his hand harder, panic digging in. The thought of bonding with End flashed in my mind. I'd been able to keep Kingston here. Stopped him from slipping away. Maybe I could do the same for Ender.

"Don't even think about it," he croaked.

I tried my best to make my face a blank mask. "What?"

"Keep those pretty little teeth away from me. When I bond

with you, it's going to be because we both want it. Not because of some ridiculous ploy to keep me here."

I bared my teeth at him. "If you die on me, I'll never forgive you."

"I'll remember that when I haunt your ass," Ender shot back.

"That's not funny." Tears pricked the corners of my eyes.

Ender squeezed my hand. "I'm not going anywhere, Kitten."

Franco railed against the knives pinning him to the wall as he snarled and spat.

"You might want to get something else to hold him," Clara suggested. "He's not currently human."

"Then what the hell is he?" Puck demanded of his sister.

"He's got a demon controlling him through dark magic. There's a way to remove the magic and the demon, but we need to confine him until your healer arrives," Clara explained calmly.

King's eyes narrowed on her. "How do you know all this?"

Clara looked him dead in the eyes. "Because a dark mage tried to kill me."

CHAPTER THIRTY-NINE

Ender

Fuck, my shoulder hurt. The ride back to Arcane territory hadn't exactly been pleasant, even with the tonic Hera had given me for the pain. And the fact that an incapacitated Franco was in the back of the SUV hadn't helped. I felt a little better now that he was chained in the gym, but not much.

Having a threat to Wren in the same twenty-mile radius was hard for me to stomach, but having him in the same house was nearly intolerable. And I knew why. Because she'd come to mean more to me than any other being on this planet and beyond.

"Would you lay back so I can deal with your wound?" Hera demanded.

I sent a scowl her way. "I think the possessed man down the hall is a little more important right now."

Clara's guards were keeping watch, along with Clyde and Juan, and Hera had given them another tranquilizer in case Franco came around again. But, somehow, it didn't feel like enough.

"Spelled. Not possessed. Dark magic, remember?" Clara called from the corner as she flipped through Hera's grimoire, on the hunt for the right unbinding spell.

"The term doesn't matter. What does is getting the demon that wants Wren's goddamned soul out of Franco," I snarled.

"Please," Wren said quietly. "We have people working on Franco. But your wound needs healing. Lie back."

It was the slightly desperate air to her voice that had me obeying. As if I'd do anything to avoid causing Wren more pain—because I'd caused too much already.

I reclined on the medical gurney set up so my torso was raised in a half-sitting position. Hera moved in closer, Locke at her side, playing assistant. "Wren, grip his hand," the healer instructed. "This is going to hurt like hell, and it'll help if he has you as a tether."

Kingston eyed Hera. "You really think that's a good idea?"

Wren's throat worked as she swallowed, but she instantly took my hand in both of hers. "It's not your choice."

I could feel the raised skin of the scars around her wrists, marks I now knew came from being shackled by her monster of a father. I breathed through that reminder and focused on Wren.

Her wildflower and rain scent that teased my nose. The slightly raised calluses surrounded by smooth, silky skin. Everything about Wren was complex. Nothing simple and easy to understand. She was the type of woman you discovered layer by layer and were constantly surprised by what you found.

Hera met my gaze as she held the damn ceremonial bowl. "Ready?"

"Can't wait," I said wanly.

"Don't be a chicken," Puck muttered. "You've had way worse than this."

One corner of Brix's mouth kicked up. "Remember when the hawk shifter took a chunk out of your neck?"

"Or when the grizzly shifter got your hindquarters?" King reminded me. "You couldn't sit down for two weeks straight."

"Enough, boys," Hera muttered. "Three, two—" She didn't wait for one. Didn't let me brace. She poured the concoction onto my wound, letting it flood the oozing opening and spill out, running down the rest of my body.

Lights flashed in front of my eyes as the pain took hold, an agony so vicious that it stole the air right from my lungs. My wolf let out a howl, and some part of me was aware that my human half echoed the sound.

"Hold him down!" Hera shouted.

Strong hands gripped me, pressing me into the hard mattress, keeping me in place. Wren's hand gripped mine harder. "Breathe, Ender. Just breathe. Hold on. You're getting through it. Your wound is being cleaned so it can heal. Just keep breathing."

Something about her voice held me there, kept me from fading.

Hera began chanting, and the pain shifted, not lessening exactly, but the quality changed. It went from sheer, blinding agony to burning pain as if pieces were being burned right out of me. And maybe they were—the infected ones, the bits where dark magic had gotten a foothold.

My vision tunneled, but I could still see the concoction Hera had poured over me, lifting now. It glowed. But within the glow was darkness. A smoky, inky void that had been inside me.

Hera chanted louder, and then an explosion sounded. And then...it was gone. All of it simply vanished, and I collapsed back against the bed, breathing heavily. Panting. Struggling to get air.

But then Wren's forehead pressed to my temple. "You did it. You made it through."

"I feel like someone exploded a bomb in my chest," I croaked.

"Kind of looks like someone did, too," Brix muttered.

Wren straightened, sending him a scathing look. "Not helping."

Brix held up both hands. "I don't think lying is gonna help."

"I'm fixing it," Hera muttered, sounding exhausted all of a sudden. She painted a salve on my chest that smelled sweet, almost comforting. But that comfort died when she lit the damn stuff on fire.

"What the fuck?" Brix snarled.

"Holy hell," Locke rasped.

I blinked up at her. "It doesn't hurt. It feels…good."

Hera sent me a tired smile. "It's restoring you."

The flames danced in a bluish color before snuffing out and revealing completely healed muscle and skin. The only thing left was a small star mark on my shoulder.

"A reminder of what you survived," Hera said softly.

Wren clasped my hand tighter. "How do you feel?"

I did a mental sweep. The pain was completely gone. I felt a little sore and tired, but not nearly as much as I should be. "I feel good," I told her honestly.

Relief swept through Wren, her shoulders slumping as tension fled. Air left her lungs with a whoosh. "Thank the gods."

"And you need to rest," Clara ordered, guiding Hera to a chair. "Drink this. It's a blend my healer has found helps replenish both her magical and human stores."

Hera collapsed into the chair. "Thank you."

Clara tapped the open grimoire. "I found the spell. But it'll take more out of Hera, and she needs to rest first."

Locke studied the page in the book. "You're sure it's dark mages?"

It was Hera who answered. "Yes. The spell I just performed only works on dark magic. That's why it exhausted me so much. Dark magic takes the greatest toll."

King muttered a curse and ran a hand through his dark hair. "One more enemy back in the picture."

But it was so much worse than that. Because if they were after Wren specifically, and in a way that would harness her soul and powers, it meant only one thing. I met Wren's gaze. "They know you're an empath."

CHAPTER FORTY

Wren

THE ONLY PEOPLE WHO REMAINED IN THE MEDICAL ROOM were our pack. Our bond. Clara was clucking over our healer, ensuring Hera took a nap before tackling the spell that would free Franco from whatever had a hold of him. In the meantime, Clara's guards and our human contingent were keeping watch. And given how powerful this dark magic was, I didn't think it was a bad idea.

I handed Ender the restorative tonic Hera always recommended, and he drank it down without argument. I watched as his throat worked, tracking the movement of the drink into his body. My gaze stayed riveted on his chest—the planes of muscle dotted with ink and now the single star that marked this experience.

"At least you got a badass scar for your troubles," Puck said as he sat on one of the stools. While his tone was light, I'd seen the worry in his gaze—in the gaze of all my guys.

As they argued about who had the best scars, my eyes lifted, finding Ender's amber orbs locked on me. Pressure built behind my eyes. "You stepped in front of a blade for me."

Ender didn't look away. "Yes."

There was only one thing I wanted to know. One thing I *needed* to know more than my next breath. "Why?"

Ender still didn't look away. Gold sparks flitted through his amber irises as he stared back at me. "You know why."

My breath caught in my throat. "Tell me anyway."

The room went silent around us—the guys realizing this was our tipping point. The one where Ender could come to terms with everything we all shared or run from it like he'd done for so long.

Those sparks intensified as he reached out. His hand slid along my jaw and into my hair. "Because I love you. Because you're mine, and I'm yours. Even when I didn't want it to be so. Because your soul is forever tethered to mine, and I wouldn't want it any other way."

There was nothing then. No sound, sight, or scent. Nothing but Ender. He was everywhere and in everything. And suddenly, I was drowning in him.

The grip of Ender's hand on my hair sent sparks cascading through my scalp, into my neck, and down my spine. The scent of leather and spice swirled around me and embedded in my skin, making me tingle with what we could be. And as I looked into those amber depths, I saw nothing but truth. Nothing but love.

"Ender," I croaked.

His free hand lifted and traced my bottom lip. "I love how strong you are. How you never back down, never give up. I love how kind you are, always seeing who needs something and coming alongside them in the perfect way. I love how fiery you are. How you never let a single soul get away with what they shouldn't. Even me."

Ender's hand dropped, his arm encircling me and lifting me onto the gurney so I straddled him. "The fact that I hurt you will haunt me for the rest of my days. But I will do everything I can to make amends. To make sure that you know how much I love you. I'll worship you with all I have and all that I am."

I framed his face with my hands, bending and letting my lips hover above his. "It's forgiven. I see you. For who you really are. You use your brutality in an effort to protect the ones you love. I'm never going to begrudge you that."

Ender shook his head. "You've made me see the world in more than black and white, more than shades of gray, more than color itself. You've made me see what lies beneath. And I won't ever stop looking for it now."

"Fucking finally," Puck muttered.

Kingston slapped him upside the head. "You're ruining the moment."

"But it doesn't mean he isn't happy as hell for you. We all are," Brix amended.

"Let's leave them be," Locke said softly, but I could see the love shining in his eyes.

"Don't," Ender rasped, his eyes searching mine before moving to his brothers. "Stay."

"End..." Kingston began.

"It should be all of us as we've always been meant to be," I rasped.

Kingston moved to the side of the gurney, his fingers threading through my hair. "Nothing would give me more pleasure than watching our bond fully become one. Than seeing my brother take you. And you, him."

Wetness rushed between my thighs at just the images King's words filled my mind with. My mouth met Ender's, even as Kingston's hand stayed tangled in my hair. I swallowed every word Ender had given me and burned them into my bones.

Ender pulled back but still held me to him. "I want to be yours. I want you to be mine."

"I want the same." My voice was more rasp than words, but he heard me, nonetheless.

Those amber eyes bled to pure gold. "Do you trust me?"

That was the ultimate question. The one we couldn't get past without a specific answer. But now? Now, I knew I could give it to him freely.

"Yes."

There was no waiting. Claws lengthened from his fingertips, and he shredded my shirt, my bra right along with it. But he didn't stop there. His claws moved to my workout leggings, and he shredded them, too.

I could do nothing but gape at the man beneath me. "You didn't."

Ender's grin was completely wolfish as he gazed up at me. "Nothing can keep me from you now, Kitten."

"Ruining a perfectly good outfit, End? How could you?" Puck all but purred as he stepped into my side, running his nose along my neck until it reached one of my marks.

Ender shot up, taking a nipple into his mouth and sucking deeply. My back arched as a moan slipped free. Ender's hand slid between my thighs, and he groaned around my nipple. "So fucking wet, and we've barely touched you."

His words had done it. The promise of him, of all we could be. Two fingers slid inside me, and my core tightened around him. He swirled those fingers, making a shudder race through me as he pulled my nipple deeper into his mouth.

"Look how well you're taking his fingers, Little Warrior," Brix growled as he stroked himself through his pants.

"Look at the way her back arches," Locke whispered, running a hand down my spine. "Owning every ounce of her pleasure."

Ender's fingers swirled inside me, sending my mouth into a silent O. But I wanted to speak. Needed to give him something. "Ender." It was the only thing I could say because I was drowning again. In the feeling of him, and knowing that he would be mine. It was almost more than I could take.

His lips released that hard peak and his free hand collared my throat. "My name on your lips. There's no better sound."

My walls tightened around Ender's fingers as I whimpered.

"Please," I begged. "I need to feel all of you. Filling me. Stretching me. Truly making me yours."

A cacophony of growls filled the air and sent vibrations through me, only heightening everything.

"Help me make it more," Ender snarled. "Help me make it everything."

"Our fucking pleasure," Kingston growled.

His mouth took mine, tongue stroking in as Puck's lips closed around one nipple, working the bud into a hard peak. A moment later, I felt Locke at my other breast, his teeth grazing my sensitive flesh.

But then Ender's fingers were gone, and I whimpered all over again. A burn lit inside me, one I knew only he could tend. And it would burn so much brighter with the rest of our bondmates with us.

Ender's hips lifted as he shucked his pants and boxer briefs. The moment they hit the floor, his eyes locked with someone behind us. "Brother. It's always been you and me. Let us cement forever the same way."

I heard movement behind me, the sound of Brix ridding himself of clothing as King's mouth tore from mine, his eyes hooded.

Brix's hands tightened on my hips, gripping and lifting as he climbed onto the gurney. Ender moved at the same time, kneeling so I was pinned between the two men and surrounded by King, Locke, and Puck.

Everyone moved as one, their mental link and bond creating a seamless wave of sensation. Lips closing around each nipple. King's hand in my hair, pulling for just a bit of bite as Brix's fingers slid between my thighs.

"Dripping," he growled, spreading that wetness to the tight, puckered hole behind.

My whole body shuddered in the most delicious way. At the promise of what was to come. But mostly at the knowledge that I would be theirs, and they would be mine. All of them.

I cupped Ender's face, bleeding everything there weren't words for into the touch.

"Give me the words, Kitten. Again."

"Ender." My eyes locked with his. "Make me yours. All of yours."

And they did.

Ender thrust into me, not gently, but in a way that said he trusted that I could handle all his power, all that was him. My mouth fell open as my eyelids fluttered at the stretch, the pressure, the hint of pain.

"Don't close your eyes. Don't let me lose you. I need to see. All of you." Alpha vibes bled into Ender's voice, showing me just how strong he truly was, all he held back from most of the world.

My eyes flew open, and I didn't lose the gold this time.

"Brother," Ender growled. And then I felt Brix at my backside, easing into me with tiny thrusts.

"Fucking hell," Brix uttered, his words strangled. "Push back, Wren."

"Let him in, Birdie," Puck coached. "So beautiful. Taking them both. Taking what only they can give you."

And he was right. Because of what they'd endured together, there was a special bond between them. And I knew Ender wouldn't have survived all these years without Brix. But it was more. It was just one more example of how we all made each other better and fit together in ways the universe had destined.

So, I let them in. Both at once, in a cadence that was only theirs. Joined by men who strung every nerve ending in me higher. Locke's teeth grazed my nipple as King nipped at my neck. Puck sucked a bud deep, and King's finger played with my clit.

Ender powered into me on thrusts that had my back bowing and claws lengthening. And Brix answered every charge with one of his own.

"Mark me," Ender snarled. "Show the world I'm yours."

My claws raked down his chest, blood blooming in a way I

knew meant he'd carry the scars forever. But the flash of pain, of claiming, only spurred him on. Ender's thrusts picked up speed and power, Brix's following in answer.

My inner walls fluttered around them both, pulsing in waves that meant I wouldn't be able to hold out for long.

The gold in Ender's eyes flashed harder. "Now!" he barked.

My fangs pressed through my gums as my head shot forward, and I bit down on Ender's neck. His fangs clamped down on a spot just above my heart. The bond didn't spark this time. It blazed. I wasn't sure whether it was because we'd held back for so long or because he was my final mate.

But I was wholly engulfed in a blaze of pleasure and need. Ender took me with a fervor I'd never felt before. The lights flickered above and then burst, sending glass and sparks shattering around the room. But none of us cared. I only felt teeth and tongues and desperate need.

We took and gave, losing ourselves in all that was us. Until my body finally gave out altogether and I collapsed onto Ender. But I did it knowing he'd always be there to catch me. They all would.

CHAPTER FORTY-ONE

Wren

I BLINKED AGAINST THE LIGHT AS IT FILTERED IN THROUGH gauzy window coverings. But I didn't recognize them. What I *did* recognize was the scent. It wrapped around me in the most comforting embrace, just like the arms that echoed the sentiment.

Ender's lips brushed my shoulder. "How do you feel, mate?"

I smiled so widely it almost hurt. "Amazing. But don't let that go to your head."

He chuckled, rolling me to face him. "I love you."

"I love you, too." My fingers traced the mark that now rested on Ender's neck. An arrow straight through a heart, realistic but somehow not grotesque. "It's perfect," I whispered.

He shivered in pleasure. "Careful, Kitten. You keep doing that, and we won't leave this bed for hours, and I have a feeling you'll want to see Franco now that he's free."

I jerked upright. "He is? Hera's spell worked?"

Ender's gaze dropped to my bare chest, staying there. He didn't answer.

I lifted the sheet to cover myself. "Cat Daddy?"

His lips twitched. "Sorry. You're too beautiful for your own good."

My mouth curved. "Franco..."

"King says he's good. Tired, but recovering. No signs of the dark magic. But we'll need you to interact with him to test it." Tension wound around each word, and I knew Ender wasn't crazy about the idea.

I reached out and stroked his stubbled cheek. "I'll be safe."

"Damn right, you will be. Because I'll be at your side."

I kissed him quickly. "All right."

Since our bond was so new, it would be difficult for him to even allow our fellow bondmates around us, let alone someone who'd tried to kill me yesterday. My hand dropped to Ender's. "Do you have some clothes I can borrow?"

A small smile pulled at Ender's lips. "I *do* like the idea of you wearing my clothes, my scent all over you."

"I'm pretty sure your scent is in my skin at this point."

Ender leaned forward, running his nose down the column of my neck. "Yes...it is." He growled and nipped me playfully.

"Clothes, now. Sexy times, later."

He let out a growl but forced himself away from me. "All right." He stood and hauled me over his shoulder, slapping my ass. "Let's cover this perfect backside before I decide to keep you chained in my room for the rest of the day."

I giggled as he carried me toward the closet. "You know, this room isn't really what I expected."

"How so?"

"It's all peaceful neutrals and gorgeous impressionist landscapes."

Ender set me down in the closet. "What did you expect?"

I shrugged. "A lot of black and the skulls of your kills?"

Ender snorted. "I save that for my armory room."

"You mean your pussy palace and armory room?"

He groaned. "Don't say pussy. You're going to make me hard, and I need to focus on dark magic and demons."

I choked on a laugh. "Sorry?"

"You damn well should be."

I grinned as we got dressed. I looked ridiculous in a pair of Ender's sweats and a tee, but I couldn't deny that I loved the scent of leather and spice being that much closer. As we headed for the door, I felt a slight pressure in my mind, as if someone were asking for entry.

The pressure built behind my eyes, and my nose stung as I looked up at Ender. "Pack bonds?"

He nodded, his smile soft.

It had been so long since I'd felt the mind-speak that came with being a pack member. I could've been blooded in at some point, meaning Kingston and I would've combined blood, and I would've sworn loyalty. But that wasn't a good idea when you were partially mated to members of an existing pack. It could mess with the bond mojo. But now that I was bonded to all of Arcane, I was automatically a part of them.

I lowered my mental shields, and Ender's voice filled my mind. *"We're coming down."*

"We're all here," Kingston answered through mind-speak. *"Including Franco."*

"Is he okay?" I asked.

"Love hearing you here," Kingston purred through my thoughts. *"And, yes. Physically, he's fine. Emotionally, he's still processing. I think it will help for him to see you."*

That spurred me on. I hurried out the door and down the stairs, the sound of voices pulling me toward the kitchen. But before I could get there, Ender caught my arm.

"Careful, Kitten. We take this nice and easy."

"He's not going to hurt me."

"No, he's not. But we also don't know how he'll react. Slow and steady."

I scowled at the floor but let Ender go ahead of me. As we stepped into the kitchen, all the voices went silent. People were spread out at the large kitchen table and the island. But I only had eyes for Franco.

He was perched on a stool, gripping a cup of what looked like tea. His hair was in disarray, and he had dark circles under his eyes. But those eyes were locked on me.

Franco straightened and poised to rise, but Ender held out a hand to stop him. "Just stay there for now."

"End," I hissed. "He's fine."

Franco shook his head. "No, he's right. We need to see how I react." Franco braced as if expecting himself to launch into the air and go on the attack all over again.

One minute passed, and then another.

"Do you sense any negative emotions?" Hera asked.

I shook my head. "Nothing. He feels exactly like he always has."

The tension in Ender's shoulders eased a fraction. "All right."

But Franco still didn't move. "What if I try to hurt you again?"

I shoved Ender out of the way and crossed to my friend—one of the first I'd made in Crescent Creek. I took his hand and squeezed. "You won't."

Clara set her coffee on the island. "You weren't yourself. But you are now. They don't have a hold of you anymore."

Franco's throat worked as he struggled to swallow. "I get these flashes of memory. All I could think was that I needed to stab you in the heart."

"It wasn't you. It was the dark mages," I told him, wishing I could boot all of them to the depths of hell where they belonged.

Franco shook his head. "They all explained, but it just…it doesn't seem real."

"Dude," Juan said before shoveling a bite of waffle into his mouth. "They turn into fuckin' wolves. The tall one's a vampire. It's possible."

Rhys's lips twitched. "Thanks for noticing."

Puck smacked him upside the head.

Franco's gaze came back to me. "Tell me what we need to do to defeat them."

CHAPTER FORTY-TWO

Wren

"Oh, hell no," Puck said, pushing to his feet from his spot at the kitchen table. "You can't be involved with this."

Franco stood with enough force to send his stool rocking. "I'm already a part of it. They brainwashed me."

"Spelled you," Clara corrected, taking another sip of coffee.

"Whatever. They messed with my head and made me try to *kill* one of my best friends. That's going to haunt me for the rest of my days," Franco snapped.

Guilt washed through me. It was my fault that this had happened to him. *My* choice to have friends in the human world. My power and gifts the dark mages were after.

"Don't," Locke said, moving to my side as he picked up on my thoughts. "This isn't on you."

Clara's gaze moved to me as Locke pulled me into his arms.

"He's right," she began. "I took you as someone with brains, and it would be moronic to take the actions of the dark mages on yourself."

I stared back at her. "You said they tried to kill you."

She sent me a tired smile. "Fun times."

"Don't joke," Puck clipped.

"Relax, Pucker. I'm fine." But she lifted her shirt to reveal a star mark similar to Ender's. "My attacker missed my heart, and I was able to...incapacitate him."

"You mean kill him," Franco cut in.

Clara winced. "Yes. But we didn't know him. What he was or what had happened to him. Not until I researched the blade."

"What were they trying to get from you?" Kingston asked. That was a damn good question.

"Alpha," Eliza warned.

Clara held up a hand to quiet her. "They have entrusted us with their secrets. I can do the same." She steeled her shoulders. "What Eliza did to the humans at the gym... That was my gift, passed to her because she is one of my enforcers. I can share it with those I have a blood bond with. It only works on the human race, but I can impact their minds. Tell them what to do."

I shared a look with my bondmates. Dark magic could create the same effect, but it required a great sacrifice. If the dark mages had Clara's power, they would no longer need that. They'd be able to make an entire army.

"Are they still hunting you?" Puck demanded.

Clara smiled, but it was a cold one. "I killed every member of their coven. They will not come for me again."

I shivered. While it might've been necessary, I still ached for the loss of life.

"This coven, the one that spelled Franco, they know about Wren and her empath gifts," Kingston said, his voice going hard. "We'll have to take them on as well as Red River."

The sheer number of people was beyond daunting. Even with Clara and her guards helping, it would be nearly impossible.

Clyde stood from his chair and sauntered toward King. "It looks like you'll be needing us."

"Clyde—"

"Listen here, boy. You're as close to a son as I've had, and I'm not about to let you get slaughtered because you're outmanned and outgunned," Clyde clipped. "We may not be some super species, but maybe that's exactly what these monsters won't expect."

Kingston went quiet as he mulled that over. "You might have a point there."

Juan popped a piece of egg casserole into his mouth. "You won't keep us out. We'll just keep meddling." He glanced at Clara. "And don't think about using that mind meld mumbo jumbo on us, hottie."

Hera's lips twitched. "I actually have something that will protect you all from supernatural mind control." She fished in her pocket and came out with four amber amulets on leather cords. "Here." She began handing them out, but when she reached Clyde, she gave him two. "For your Dina."

Clyde's smile was soft. "Thank you."

"Are you sure about this?" Brix asked King. "They don't have the same protections we do."

"I—"

King's words were cut off as Rhys grabbed the counter to steady himself. His eyes bled of all color, leaving them completely white.

"What's happening?" I yelled. "Is he having a seizure?"

"Don't touch him," Ender barked. "It's a vision."

We waited in pained silence as Rhys's entire form looked like it had been struck by lightning. And then he suddenly collapsed.

Ender cursed, rushing in to catch him before he hit the floor. Rhys's chest heaved as he struggled to catch his breath. "Thank you," he wheezed.

I stared at the vampire, who was clearly still in pain. "Is that what happens every time you have a vision?"

His gaze cut to me. "Not all sunshine and rainbows, Little Vixen. It's why I normally try to avoid them like the plague."

My brow furrowed. "Can you stop them from coming?"

Rhys nodded. "I have to take certain herbs, but then I don't get information that could be helpful. It's a difficult balance to strike."

He was forcing himself to live through this pain for Ender. For all of us. I moved closer, taking his hand and squeezing. "Thank you. For everything you're doing."

Rhys's gaze locked with mine. "You're welcome." He squeezed my hand in return, and images filled my mind as he did. Rhys running through the woods. Pain blooming, blood seeping from his chest.

"What happened to you?" I rasped.

Rhys jerked his hand from mine. "Nothing. Not a damn thing."

But I'd felt the pain. The sheer devastation pouring out of him. Something had happened to Rhys, and it was something horrific.

CHAPTER FORTY-THREE

Wren

RHYS PULLED ON HIS MASK IN A WAY THAT SPOKE OF A seasoned actor. His gaze moved to Clyde, a wry smile tugging at his lips. "The humans need to stay."

Kingston straightened and prowled toward Rhys. "What did you see?"

Rhys showed no signs of intimidation. "I told you, it's not exact. Images, warnings. It's clear that things will go better if they're here."

"Told ya," Juan said from his spot at the table. He leaned back in his chair and patted his stomach. "Plus, the food here is sick."

Puck arched a brow at that. "Thanks?"

Juan grinned. "Totally a compliment, Pucker."

Puck bared his teeth. "*You* are definitely not allowed to call me that."

I crossed to him, looping my arm through his and leaning into his side. "Come on, buddy. No bloodshed at breakfast."

"Pucker. Buddy. What the hell did I do to deserve this?" he grumbled.

"Oh, you did plenty," Clara called. "How about when you disrupted every date I ever went on growing up?"

"Buddy, you didn't." I raised my eyebrows in mock affront.

Puck's cheeks pinked. "They didn't deserve you."

Clara pinned him with a hard look. "You ran Beckham up a flagpole. You told Glinda you'd put her on bathroom duty for the rest of time."

Puck turned to his sister, taking me with him. "And if they truly loved you as they should've, they would've taken my threats and kept right on running toward you."

Clara's jaw went slack. "You were testing them?"

"Yes. And I'd do it all over again."

"Brothers," Clara huffed.

I couldn't help it, I laughed. And then I squeezed Puck's arm harder. "You're a good big brother."

"Sometimes," he said wistfully, a hint of sadness creeping into his eyes.

Clara met his gaze across the kitchen. "All the time."

An ache settled in my chest, but it was the good kind. One that spoke of restoration and reconnection. And I was happy as hell that Puck was finding it.

"I've got a question," Clyde said, taking a sip of coffee.

"Is it about the mermaids?" Juan asked. "Because I still want to know about that."

Clyde sent him a withering stare. "No, it's not about mermaids."

"Damn."

"Jesus," King muttered, scrubbing a hand over his face.

Clyde turned to our alpha. "Do you think there's a good chance the dark mages and Red River will attack here? Or will they try for something more public?"

Kingston mulled that over for a moment. "The last time the

mages attacked, it was public, but…not. They waited until everyone but us had cleared out of the gym. And Red River, they hit in disguises. But now, they know we'll be on guard for that."

Clyde nodded slowly. "If you don't all gather in one spot outside of this property, you might be able to force them to attack here."

I frowned at the man who'd become like a father to me. "And what would that get us?"

A grin spread across his face. "You guys have all the supernatural and high-tech stuff handled, but that doesn't mean there isn't room for more defense. I think we should add a low-tech line."

Kingston nodded. "It's not a bad idea. That's not something either party would expect."

"I could position myself with a good vantage point of the traps," Ender suggested. "Take them out as they hit each one."

My stomach dropped as I thought about Ender alone in some sniper's nest. I moved to him on instinct. "It won't take them long to figure out where you are, and they will try to take you down."

End wrapped his arms around me and breathed deeply. "I have ways of escape."

"And I can be backup," Franco offered. "I'm a damn good shot. My dad's into target shooting."

Ender arched a brow but nodded. "All right."

Locke took a sip of his drink and then adjusted his glasses. "I can put sensors on the traps to let us know when one is tripped. It'll be another early warning system."

Kingston clapped his hands together. "I think we've got a plan. Let's pair off and get started."

"Wren," Hera said, rising gracefully from her seat. "I think we should check the wards. See if we can reinforce them."

Ender's grip on me tightened. "If you're going that close to the territory boundary, I'm coming with you."

One corner of Hera's mouth tugged up. "Come along, Cat Daddy."

Ender jerked back, sending me an accusing look. "You told her?"

I grinned. "I don't know. It's pretty obvious that you're king of the pussy palace."

Franco choked on a sip of tea, and Puck thumped him on the back. "Don't worry. You'll get used to it."

Ender cursed as his shovel hit another rock, and Hera let out a soft snicker.

"I heard that," Ender called from the pit he and Franco were currently digging.

"I don't care," Hera singsonged.

That had my lips twitching. Ender and Franco had been working on a trap for almost two hours already. The hope was that we could force any intruders that made it past the wards toward one of those by our camera placement. If an intruder was smart enough to make it past the energy field and the metaphysical wards, they'd likely be on the lookout to avoid any cameras, as well. And we'd have traps in each of those spots.

"You know," Franco yelled. "You could help."

"We're quite fine up here," Hera assured him.

Ender hit another rock and cursed again. I had to bite my lip to keep from laughing this time.

"Okay," Hera said. "What do you sense from the ward?"

I lowered to the ground and sat cross-legged, holding my palms to the ward. The moment they connected, the air in front of me sort of rippled. But I frowned. We'd reinforced them not that long ago, but this one felt…weaker somehow.

My brows pulled together. "It's not as strong as it should be."

"I feared as much," Hera said, pulling her grimoire out of her bag and flipping through the pages.

"Why?" I pressed.

"Magic is all about balance. Give and take. Too many beings wish you and your pack harm. Even though they aren't actively trying to break through the wards each day, they'll still drain them."

I tugged the corner of my lip into my mouth and worried it between my teeth. "How do we stop it?"

"We can't," Hera told me honestly. "For now, we simply reinforce." She fished in her bag for something.

"Do you have a whole magical grocery store in there?"

Hera chuckled. "You never know what you might need." She offered me a stone that was rock on the outside and a beautiful crystal inside. "This will help feed the ward."

As she handed it to me, our fingers brushed, and Hera stilled. Then her hand moved to my forehead, and she pressed her palm there.

"What?" I asked. "What's wrong?"

Hera glanced around furtively, her voice dropping so low I could barely hear it. "I can feel a shift in your energy. Your heat is coming."

Panic swept through me like an icy inferno. "It's not due for months."

She sent me a sympathetic smile but kept her voice quiet. "You've bonded with your final mate. It can send a signal to your body that it's time."

"I'm not ready for pups," I squeaked.

"Just breathe," Hera encouraged, then dug through her bag again. "I've got some herbs that will protect against that."

I took the small capsules and swallowed them quickly. "Is there something to keep it from coming on altogether?" I asked hopefully.

She squeezed my hand. "I'm sorry. Nothing can keep a heat from coming if you're healthy."

Fear struck in the deepest recesses of my mind, memories of all the threats Bastian had hurled at me rising. If he got me while my heat was in place, my life would be over. Or worse, I'd wish it was.

CHAPTER FORTY-FOUR

Locke

MY FINGERS FLEW ACROSS THE KEYBOARD, BUT THE steady clickety-clack of the keys didn't bring the comfort it usually did. My hand moved to the mouse as I selected the next grouping of sensors and then moved back to the keyboard. But it didn't matter how many I put in place or how many cameras searched the woods for signs of movement; none of it felt like enough.

I tipped back the last sip of my energy drink and threw it into my recycling with more force than necessary. As this one flew in, other cans flew out, and I muttered a curse.

"Should I be concerned about your caffeine intake over the past week?" Kingston asked from the doorway.

I swiveled my chair around to face him. "Sleep hasn't exactly been my friend lately."

That had him moving deeper into the lair and sitting on the couch. "Want to talk about it?"

Gods, he was a good friend. And an amazing leader. King was as different as night and day from my alpha growing up. He had prized physical strength and dominance—just one of the reasons my parents had kicked me out when they realized I was submissive.

I twisted my neck to the side, making the bones crack. "I'm okay. Really."

King simply stayed quiet and waited.

I sighed. "It feels like no matter what I do, it won't be enough."

He nodded slowly. "I feel the same. Things have changed since we found Wren. There's a hell of a lot more at stake than there was a few months ago."

"It feels like there's a boulder on my chest, pressing down, making it hard to breathe. I have to force myself to walk away from her at times because I want her to be in my sight twenty-four-seven."

One corner of Kingston's mouth pulled up. "I'd like to implant a tracker in her, just in case."

I winced.

King's brows flew up. "Tell me you didn't."

"No, no. I gave her a necklace."

"The lock one?"

Of course, Kingston would've noticed it.

"Yes. It's enchanted, so only Wren or one of her mates can remove it, and it has a tracker inside," I admitted. "I told her it did. It's not like I'm tracking her without her permission."

King lifted a hand to still me. "I'm not accusing you. I wish I would've thought of it."

"Sometimes, when we're apart, I just watch her location. I have the app up while I'm working, just for reassurance."

Kingston leveled an alpha stare at me. "It's completely understandable. She's been taken from us twice."

Just hearing the words had my fingers twitching to pick up my phone and check the app. "It feels like a compulsion. And the panic…"

"It won't be like this forever," King assured me. "It's a unique circumstance. Once we've dealt with the dark mages and Red River, we'll be able to breathe."

"Unless the mages told someone about her empath status." I realized that I'd just given voice to one of my greatest fears. That we'd always be running because Wren's empath status would be known to the world. Everyone under the sun would want to get their hands on her.

Kingston shook his head. "We can't lose logic. How would telling anyone benefit them?"

I thought that over for a moment. "It wouldn't. It would only give them competition."

"Exactly. We end them. We end the threat."

Something eased in me for the first time in days. "You're right."

King's lips twitched. "Might want to record that for posterity."

I chuckled, shaking my head. "Don't get used to it."

"Come on," he said, pushing to his feet. "Dinner's ready, and you need to balance out some of that caffeine."

He wasn't wrong. As I stood, I could feel the jitteriness in my limbs. Never a good sign. "Maybe some juice with dinner."

Kingston barked out a laugh. "I don't think I've ever seen you have anything but soda or coffee at *any* meal."

"There always has to be a first, right?"

He clapped me on the back as we headed down the hall. "Damn straight."

I looked up at the sound of footsteps. Wren walked down the stairs, her hair still damp from a shower. She wore a flowy dress with delicate straps and flowers cast over the fabric. It reminded me of her scent: wild and free.

"You look beautiful," I greeted.

Pink hit her cheeks. "Thank you."

I brushed my lips over hers as she reached the bottom step. She returned the kiss but ended it quickly and put some distance between us. I frowned. That wasn't like Wren. She always welcomed simple touches, the ones that connected us.

"Better get in there. Dinner's ready," she said, hurrying away.

I glanced at Kingston, who was frowning after her. "That was weird, right?"

He nodded. "Her wolf might be on edge with so many people in the house."

"Maybe." But that didn't seem right. She'd been fine this morning.

I wound my way into the dining room, which was already packed with people, and made a beeline for the open seat next to Wren. She shifted slightly as I sat, looking almost uncomfortable.

"Are you okay?" I whispered.

Wren glanced my way for a moment before looking back at the food at the center of the table. "Of course."

That only had my frown deepening.

"Okay, everyone," Puck said, calling us all to order. "I have been working all afternoon on this feast, so you'd better appreciate it."

Everyone laughed.

"You know I will," Juan said, patting his stomach.

Puck just shook his head and picked up a glass of wine. "To my sister. Thank you for coming all this way and for always having my back. I love you."

Everyone raised their glasses and echoed sentiments of welcome. We dove into the Italian feast Puck had created. There was pasta, gnocchi, meatballs, chicken cacciatore, garlic bread, and Caesar salad. It was truly a feast worthy of royalty. But I would've enjoyed it a hell of a lot more if I wasn't so worried about Wren.

She was quiet through dinner, pasting on a smile when someone engaged her, but otherwise, she seemed to pull inward as if some tangle of thoughts held her captive. She nibbled at her food but didn't eat nearly enough for my liking. And as I studied her, I realized a flush had spread over her skin as the night wore on.

"Wren," I whispered, taking her hand. I'd meant to ask her if she was feeling okay, but the moment I touched her, I realized her skin was scorching. "You're burning up."

I leaned in to put a hand to her brow, but that's when I scented it. The heady edge to her wildflowers-and-rain aroma. One that had me tipping into a haze. "Heat," I rasped. "You're in heat."

The whole room froze.

CHAPTER FORTY-FIVE

Wren

ENERGY CRACKLED THROUGH THE AIR AT LOCKE'S WORDS, but I couldn't find it in me to care. My head swam, and my skin felt like I'd laid out under the blistering sun for far too long. Everything in me hurt.

I'd only been through a heat a handful of times in my life, but it had never been this bad before. Normally, I took ibuprofen and called off work for a couple of days, but that was it. Now, I felt like I was dying.

It was Ender who moved first. He knocked his chair back, striding around the table and lifting me from mine.

I let out a moan of half pain, half pleasure. Just the feeling of his arms around me felt as if every nerve ending had awoken, including ones I didn't even know I had.

Ender cursed as some part of me became aware of Franco asking what was wrong. But his voice sounded so far away.

"Get her upstairs," King barked.

That voice was closer, and I wanted more of it. I wanted to feel the vibrations against my skin like endless fingertips.

I twisted in Ender's arms and cried out.

"Holy hell," Puck swore. "How did we miss this?"

"We've had a few other things on our plate," King shot back.

A new hand brushed my cheek as we climbed the stairs. "It'll be okay, Little Warrior," Brix vowed. "We'll take care of you."

I twisted again, so uncomfortable in my skin but needing more of Brix, more of his promises and comfort.

"We need to make sure she's taken something," Locke said softly. "We can't be reckless with her."

"Hera," I croaked. "Gave…me…herbs." Each word felt nearly impossible to speak but I somehow managed to get them out.

"She could've given us some warning," Ender spat. "We could've had time to prepare."

"You know we'd never have been able to prepare for her first mated heat. It's always the strongest. We just have to see her through it," King said quietly.

Some part of me was aware of a door opening and then closing again. I recognized glimpses of our pack bedroom—the one that was truly ours. We hadn't even had a chance to all sleep in the bed as a completed bond yet.

"Locke, get some ice," Kingston ordered as Ender laid me on the bed.

I let out another moan as the duvet's cool cotton brushed against my overheated skin.

Ender cupped my face, his rough thumbs brushing the apples of my cheeks. "Killing me, Kitten."

"Hurts," I whispered.

"We're going to take the pain away, Birdie. I promise." A second later, Puck ripped my dress down the middle.

"I liked her in that dress," Locke called from the bar area.

"I'll buy her a new one," Puck spat.

"Fuck, she's beautiful," Brix ground out. He climbed onto the bed, his hand trailing down my neck.

Wetness gathered between my thighs, soaking the delicate lace of the boy shorts I wore. I swore I could come with just his fingers grazing my neck. My back arched as I searched for more. Though what it was, I didn't know.

"Look at the way she bends," King rasped. "Never breaking because she's so damn strong."

My breaths came in quick pants as Puck shifted between my legs. His hands slid up my thighs, making me cry out and thrust my hips upward. "Baby," he whispered. "I've got you."

Ender gripped my hips, holding them as Brix slid two pillows under them. The position had me completely on display as Puck's claws shredded the sides of my underwear. He tugged the lace free and let out a low growl. "Your scent. It'll bring me to my knees every time."

He ran his nose up one thigh until he reached the apex. His tongue lashed out, parting me and making me cry out.

Kingston moved onto the bed, his palm gliding over my belly. "She's too hot. She'll overheat. Locke, the ice."

"I've got it," he called, climbing onto the bed.

King lengthened one claw and snipped my bralette in three strategic places. It fell from my body with no effort at all. But I was too lost in Puck's tongue to care. He lapped at me as if he were a man starved. Then his tongue circled my clit, flicking that bundle of nerves.

Everything in me wound tighter as Brix's mouth met mine. His tongue drove in, giving me a whole new sensation to war with. But then the ice hit me.

Cubes ran over my collarbones and around my chest. I could feel Ender and Locke moving them in tandem, but also with rhythms entirely their own. My nipples pebbled, straining for more, and I groaned into Brix's mouth. He took and took, melding my taste with his.

The ice hit my nipples, and my back bowed even more. Agony ripped through me, and my inner walls fluttered. I needed more. Needed to be filled.

"Puck," Kingston growled. "She needs you."

In a flash, Puck's tongue was gone. I felt movement between my thighs and heard rustling as King's finger found my clit. He circled and stroked. "We've got you, Little Warrior. Just hold on."

The ice moved around my hard peaks, making them strain and tighten. Then Ender's lips closed around one, working it. The juxtaposition of that and Locke spinning the ice around the other had my hands fisting in their hair. The warring feelings spun me higher, showing me everything this bond could be.

Each of us was uniquely different but coming together to create something more.

Puck gripped my thighs, his fingers pressing so tightly they'd likely leave bruises—ones I'd wear with pride because he knew I needed it to keep me here. His tip bumped against my entrance, and then he slid in.

I cried out into Brix's mouth, reveling in the feel of the stretch, the delicious pressure. Puck retreated and thrust in again, more force behind his movements this time. Kingston circled my clit, mirroring Puck's tempo.

Each of my men worked in tandem yet gave something that was uniquely theirs. My skin crackled as Puck picked up speed. Everything, all of it was too much. My body trembled as everything in me began to tingle. The orgasm hit me like a physical force, painful as I tipped over the edge, but it was only matched by the pleasure it brought with it.

I arched and writhed, soaking up everything my mates gave me. I lost all sense of space and time. There was only feeling. Wave after wave crashed into me until I could take no more and the darkness claimed me. But there was no fear because I knew my mates were with me.

CHAPTER FORTY-SIX

Wren

"Nice and easy," Locke said softly as he helped me prop against the pillows. "Take a sip."

He held a straw to my lips, and I took a pull. The strawberries-and-cream flavor filled my mouth, and I let my eyes close. "You make the best tonics. Thank you."

He brushed a hand over my hair. "How do you feel?"

I opened my eyes and took in the room. The windows were open, letting in the fresh air, and Brix had changed the sheets while Kingston helped me shower. Everything was clearer now that the heat had passed. But I was exhausted.

"My muscles are a little sore, and I'm tired. But other than that, I'm fine."

Brix lifted one of my socked feet into his lap and began massaging. "You'll need to take it easy for a couple of days. You're recovering your strength."

I made a face, but Kingston slid his fingers through mine from his spot on the side of the bed. "He's right. You don't want to push."

"I've been cooped up for days," I argued.

Locke lifted the straw to my lips again. "This is your first heat as a mated wolf. It'll take more out of you. You don't want to injure yourself because you didn't get your rest."

The sound of bickering came from the hallway, and the door flew open.

"If you didn't make so much food, you wouldn't have needed help carrying it," Ender sniped.

Puck scowled at him. "Well, you ate a shit ton of that food this morning, so you could at least say thank you and help me carry the trays."

Ender glared back. "I needed energy after a seventy-two-hour fuck fest."

My lips twitched. "Fuck fest?"

Ender turned to me, a wry grin on his face. "I mean that respectfully, of course."

"Of course," I echoed.

"How do you feel after your shower, Birdie?" Puck crossed to the bed, lowering a tray full of eggs, biscuits, fruit, and juice.

"Good. It's nice to have clean hair."

Ender lowered a second tray onto the bed, this one ladened with pancakes, homemade donuts, and a glass of milk. Then he dropped a kiss to my head. "Smells good. New shampoo?"

"Hera mixed up some heat recovery beauty products for her," Locke explained.

I sniffed the ends of my strands. "She could seriously start a business. This stuff is amazing."

"What do you want to eat first?" Puck asked. "You need a little of everything. Carbs, fats, protein. They'll all help you recover."

I leaned forward and brushed my lips across his. "Thank you for always feeding me."

He grinned against my lips. "It's selfish. I love the sounds you make when you eat."

"Gods, please, no moans. I don't think my dick can take any more," Ender muttered as he climbed onto the bed next to me. "I'm pretty sure you broke it."

I choked on a laugh and felt my cheeks heat. "Sorry?"

Ender leaned in, kissing me soft and slow. "Kitten, it would be my favorite way to die."

"Less kissing, more eating," Puck ordered.

Ender scowled at him. "Easy for you to say. You already got your kiss."

"You snooze, you lose." Puck piled a few different things onto a plate and handed it to me. "Eat."

"Bossy much?" I asked, but my stomach rumbled as if to argue with my protest.

"He's right," Kingston said. "You need to eat."

I took a bite of the eggs along with a piece of biscuit. It was heavenly, but I managed to hold back my moan in respect of all the dicks around me. "Are there any updates on the dark mages or Bastian?"

King shook his head. "Nothing. Clara led the charge of putting in some more traps while we were…occupied."

My cheeks flushed as I took a sip of what I now realized was watermelon juice. "How are Clyde, Franco, and Juan doing?"

Ender's face twisted. "They're far too comfortable. They're playing some card game downstairs, and Clyde moved Dina in, too."

I sent him a warning look. "They're all welcome here. And it's probably safer this way."

"You know she's right," Brix said, his thumbs digging into the arch of my foot.

"If you're feeling up to it, we can take a walk around the property and see everything they've done," Locke offered.

I nodded as I swallowed a bite of pancake. "I need to stretch my muscles."

"Are you sure you're up for that?" Kingston pressed.

I sent him a look. "It was a heat, not a mortal injury."

His expression went soft as he moved closer and slid a hand over my belly. "I can't wait until this swells one day with our pups."

My heart did a stutter step at the image. For the first time in my life, I could see it. Building a family with these men. Pups running around, creating all sorts of havoc. My eyes misted over.

"You made her cry," Puck accused.

"It's the hormones," I said, waving a hand in front of my face.

King left his hand on my belly, his eyes searching. "Good tears?"

I nodded. "I never thought I'd have this. A real family. I thought I'd have to hide who I was forever."

"Kitten," Ender rasped, leaning his head against my temple.

"You all gave me what I never thought I'd be able to have." I remembered when my friend Hayden had found her mates when we were in college. She'd had no idea what had hit her. But I knew the preciousness of what she'd received. But, as happy as I'd been for her, I couldn't help the niggle of envy I'd felt along with it—and the despair at thinking I'd never find it.

"Love you, Wren," Locke whispered.

"I love you, too. All of you. You're going to make the best dads one day."

Brix's hold on my foot loosened, and he pushed to standing. "I need to go check on something."

He was gone before I could get another word out, and I was left wondering what the hell I'd said.

CHAPTER FORTY-SEVEN

Brix

MY HEART HAMMERED AGAINST MY RIBS AS PANIC PULSED through my veins. I needed out. Needed freedom. Wanted no walls fencing me in.

Laughter and shouts sounded from the living room as I hit the entryway.

"Brix, come play with us," Clara shouted.

I ignored her and headed straight for the back doors and out into the fall sunshine. The air had a cool edge to it—one I needed.

I didn't bother changing out of my clothes, I simply called on the shift, desperate to be in my wolf form. My bones cracked as muscle and sinew tore. In a split second, I was standing on four paws.

There was no waiting. I took off for the trees, needing to feel the wind in my fur and that illusive freedom. There were days I felt like more beast than man, days where it was easier to be in this form. Simpler.

There were no worries or complex fears when I was a wolf.

There was only instinct and reaction. I didn't have to wrestle with anxieties of what was to come; I simply faced them as they came.

My paws hit the ground hard. I leapt over fallen trees and dodged underbrush until I reached a spot at the creek. I jumped into the water, letting the shocking cold distract me from my swirling thoughts. I dunked my head in the stream, holding it there for one, two, three seconds.

As I lifted my head, I sucked in air, but the panic wasn't completely gone. I made the move again, trying to clear away the weight that had settled on my chest.

When I lifted my head this time, I heard footsteps in the distance. No, not footsteps, the sound of paws hitting the earth. I caught a glimpse of a dark brown wolf with a white heart over her chest.

No. I couldn't see Wren right now.

I leapt out of the creek and took off running. I should've known she would catch me. Our little warrior was fast and far nimbler than I was.

She hit me at full speed, taking us into a spilling tumble and snapping at me to make her displeasure known. I let out a low growl in answer, telling her I wanted to be left alone. But then her voice filled my head as she studied me.

"What's wrong?"

"Nothing."

Wren let out a chuff. *"Because you just bolt for no reason."*

I started walking, not running away but avoiding that astute, turquoise gaze. *"I needed air."*

She followed but didn't completely close the distance. *"Not a lie, but not exactly the truth either."*

I let out another growl, but this one wasn't aimed at her. It was aimed at me. She was right. It wasn't fair of me to bolt and keep every instinct and fear to myself. I slowed to a stop and turned to face her. *"I'm not sure I have what it takes to be a father."*

Wren stilled, those turquoise eyes widening. *"You don't want to be one?"*

I shook my head as a wave of grief hit me. *"There's nothing I'd want more. But, Wren, I…what happened to me, it broke pieces of me. I'm not sure I'll ever be* normal.*"*

"Fuck normal." Wren butted her head under my chin. *"You're perfect just as you are, and you'll give your son or daughter all that beautiful uniqueness."*

"It's not that simple. What if I have a freak-out around our kids?"

"Then you have a freak-out. We'll deal. That's why we have a bond. So we all balance each other out. We all help one another."

I wanted to believe her words, to trust them. Because nothing would make me happier than building a family with her and my brothers. But I wasn't so sure I was there. *"My family was taken from me when I was still so young. Sometimes, I feel like I didn't get to learn all I should've from my father."*

Wren pressed her body against mine, making our bond flare to life as a beautiful reminder of all we shared. *"My father was a monster, and my mother was ripped away from me early. I don't have an example from them either, not really. But I know the feelings I want to give to my children. Safety. Acceptance. Protection. Love. I know what I want to build for them because it's exactly what you and the rest of the pack have given me."*

"Wren…" My heart hammered against my ribs for a whole other reason now. Wren had been through so much, endured more than any being should ever have to. But she still saw beauty everywhere.

"You already know everything you need to." She licked the side of my face.

I curled around her, my wolf wanting nothing more than to be close to his miraculous mate. *"I love you."*

"More than you could ever know. We'll do this together. One thing at a time, and only when we're all ready."

I held her tightly to me, breathing in wildflowers and rain. *"I'm ready now."*

A laugh sounded through my mind. *"Maybe we should dispatch our long list of enemies first."*

I let out a chuff. *"Fair enough, Little Warrior. Fair enough."*

CHAPTER FORTY-EIGHT

Wren

PUCK FLIPPED A COIN, CATCHING IT ON THE BACK OF HIS hand as he stretched out at the table on the back patio. "I'm so bored, I think I'd take an attack at this point."

Brix sent him a grin that was a little feral around the edges. "I could always kick your ass in the gym."

Puck made a face. "You could try."

Three weeks had passed since the dark mages spelled Franco, and nothing had happened. Everything had been eerily quiet. None of Ender's contacts had heard any signs of movement from the dark mages or the Red River pack. And Rhys hadn't had any more visions either.

So, we'd simply been stuck in limbo.

"Maybe we need a pack run," Kingston suggested.

"I think I need a dirt bike or an ATV so I can keep up with you guys on those runs," Juan muttered from his spot on one of the chaise lounges.

Franco's lips twitched. "They'd still leave you in the dust."

My gaze moved from the two of them to a quilt spread out over the ground at the edge of the forest. Hera and Clara were bent over one of Hera's grimoires, studying something. They'd been thick as thieves the past few weeks, and I couldn't help but wonder if there was more going on there than friendship.

They both deserved that kind of happiness and more, and I could see the ways in which they'd balance each other out and make each other stronger—as every partnership should be.

Strong arms lifted me from my chair and deposited me on a lap. Locke nuzzled my neck. "What are you smiling at?"

I burrowed deeper into him, relishing the fact that there was nothing quite like a Locke hug. "Look at the two of them," I whispered.

My voice was low enough that only the shifters around me could hear. My bondmates followed my line of sight, studying the couple. Puck frowned. "I need to have a talk with Hera."

I kicked lightly at his knee. "No, you do not. You're not going to ruin this for your sister."

"I just want to make sure her intentions are good," Puck argued.

Ender scoffed as he stroked Princess's fur. "You want to threaten Hera to within an inch of her life."

"And she'll probably give you limp dick for the rest of your days if you do," Brix muttered.

"Who has a limp dick?" Juan called from the chaises.

"Puck, always Puck," Ender called.

Puck leveled Ender with a glare. "Careful. I'll go sabotage your bow collection, and then we'll see how you feel."

"You wouldn't."

"Stop being an asshole and you won't have to find out," Puck shot back.

As if she could understand all the words being said, Princess leapt from Ender's lap and onto the table. She bounded over and smacked Puck across the face, drawing a few specks of blood.

Puck's hand flew to his cheek. "That goddamned cat."

Princess darted away and jumped onto my lap. I couldn't help but laugh. "That's what you get for hurling insults at Cat Daddy."

Locke's chest began shaking beneath me.

Puck narrowed his eyes on me. "He started it."

"What are you, five?" King asked.

"Oh, his emotional maturity is barely three," Clyde said from the loveseat he shared with Dina.

"On a good day," Rhys called, striding out of the house, carrying a tray of drinks.

"What's with the ganging up on me?" Puck complained. "Clare Bear, make your guards rough them up. They're picking on me."

Clara turned and glanced at us. "Fight your own battles, Pucker."

"You should know he was planning on interfering with your love life again," I said.

Clara's eyes narrowed on her brother. "That is very risky, given that I know all your weaknesses *and* all your secrets."

Kingston chuckled. "You want to move to Crescent Creek, Clara? It'd be nice to have someone who can keep him in line."

"Sorry, but that sounds like a nightmare of a job."

"You guys are the worst," Puck muttered.

Rhys clapped him on the shoulder. "When you dish it out, you have to be prepared to take it."

Puck glared up at him. "You're one to talk."

Rhys put a hand over his heart. "Me? I never create any trouble."

The entire group grumbled at that. Rhys had needled or created problems for every single person here. It was as if he got a charge out of it. But as I studied him, I couldn't help but wonder what his story was.

Memories swirled, the images that had flashed in my mind

when I touched Rhys. Echoes of the pain and devastation rocketed through me. There was no doubt in my mind that Rhys hid his torment beneath charm and jokes, much like Puck did.

But as far as I could tell, Rhys didn't have anyone to share his burdens with. He called Ender his best friend, but the two rarely delved deeper than surface level. That had to be lonely.

Rhys clapped his hands together. "Ready for more empath training, Little Vixen?"

King instantly straightened. "No. It's her day off. She's been pushing herself to the breaking point every day for the past few weeks. You need to give her mind a chance to recover."

I shifted in Locke's lap, disrupting Princess, who let out a meow of protest and jumped down. "I could do a little."

King's gaze cut to me, a stern look sweeping over his face. But it quickly softened as he leaned closer and cupped my cheek. "You need rest just as much as training. It'll do you no good if you're exhausted when the dark mages or Red River strikes."

He had a damn good point, which only served to annoy me.

Locke started to laugh and then kissed my temple. "Has anyone ever told you that you're adorable when you're annoyed?"

"That's only making me more annoyed," I shot back.

King chuckled. "Apologies for being reasonable."

"It's honestly rude," I muttered.

Rhys made a gagging noise. "All this lovey-dovey stuff is turning my stomach. First Ender, my brother, who I thought would *never* bite the dust, is a total goner for the little vixen..."

Ender let out a low growl. "I'm not a *goner*."

Juan snickered. "You totally are."

"Then my Dina abandons me for Clyde," Rhys went on.

Dina arched a brow. "My keeping you in liquor doesn't make me yours."

"Damn straight," Clyde echoed.

Rhys just rolled his eyes. "Even those two are all coupled up." He gestured at Hera and Clara, his gaze lingering there. "Though, I would quite like to join that group. What do you say, ladies? Care to make it a throuple?"

Clara flipped him off, but Hera sent sparks flying in Rhys's direction. They hit him dead-on, and he let out a little shriek. "That hurt, oh violent one. But I get it. It's your kink."

Hera turned to Puck's sister. "Do you think he'd get that I'm not interested if I beheaded him?"

Clara shrugged. "Might want to burn the body for good measure."

"Harsh," Rhys mumbled. But the moment the word left his mouth, his body jerked, and his eyes turned pure white.

We all shot to our feet as Rhys's whole form trembled. A handful of seconds later, he stumbled forward, and Ender rushed to steady him. Rhys's eyes were wide with panic. "They're coming."

CHAPTER FORTY-NINE

Wren

The moment the words left Rhys's lips, everyone erupted. Questions were hurled from one direction and then another, everyone talking over each other.

"Enough!" Kingston ordered. The tone was pure alpha, and everyone instantly quieted. "What did you see?"

Rhys's throat worked as he swallowed. "I…it was just snapshots." His brow furrowed. "I think it's of two different times because I saw images of the dark mages and then Red River."

"Did anything clue you into a day or time?" Clara asked, her enforcers filing in around her as if she were about to be attacked here and now.

Rhys pinched the bridge of his nose, clearly in pain as he struggled to remember what he'd seen.

I turned to Locke. "Do you have any of your headache herbs?"

He nodded, pulling a packet from his pocket and handing it to me.

I crossed to the table, poured the contents into an empty glass, and then filled it with water.

"I'm not sure what day," Rhys mumbled. "But it was full daylight."

"That helps," Kingston said. "We'll know when to be more on alert."

Stirring the tonic, I handed it to Rhys. "Here. It helps with headaches."

"Thank you," Rhys said as he took the glass from me.

"It might look like the worst thing ever, but it doesn't taste half bad," I promised.

He gulped it down and then set the glass back on the table. The lines bracketing his mouth were already softening. "That does work."

"Could you tell where the attack happened?" I asked.

Rhys's lips pursed, but this time, it was because he was searching through his memories, not because he was in pain. "In the forest…here. I recognized a spot where the creek hits the wards on one side. And that huge boulder on the other."

"Did you see us fighting them?" I pressed.

Rhys shook his head. "No. Just them coming onto pack territory."

An alert, unlike anything I'd ever heard before, came from behind me. I whirled to find Locke fumbling with his phone and silencing the alarm. His fingers flew across the screen as his eyes went wide. "My power grid. It's completely down."

"How?" Kingston ground out. "Those lines run deep under our property."

Locke shook his head, but his gaze stayed focused on his phone. "It has to be by magical means, not human ones."

A pit formed in my stomach as dread bloomed. *Magical means.* It had to be the dark mages or Red River. The only question was, which one?

"What about the solar-powered cameras?" Brix demanded.

Locke's head shot up, his brows pulling together. "I might

be able to tap into their network from the satellite." His fingers flew again and then stilled. "The mages. Northwest corner. They're through the electric field and working on lowering the wards."

Hera and I shared a look. We knew the wards were already struggling to stay up with all the animosity hitting them. It wouldn't be long before they gave out altogether.

Kingston's gaze swept the group. "We all know our roles and groupings."

I swallowed hard as I reached for Ender's hand. He squeezed my fingers in answer, saying everything we didn't have time for.

"Clyde and Dina, you're in the watch room. Locke will patch you into auxiliary power and the satellite for internet. You're our eyes and ears."

They instantly headed for the house and Locke's lair.

"Ender and Franco, the sniper's nest."

They nodded, and Franco held out his fist to Ender. "Let's lock and load."

Ender tapped his knuckles to Franco's, and then they were off.

"Puck, Locke, and Juan, you're on the ground with Rhys. Hera, you're with the enforcers and Clara. Brix and Wren, you're with me," King instructed.

My mouth had gone dry as I thought about how the people I loved most were here. If we lost, everyone I loved would be wiped from this earth.

Rhys met my gaze. "Remember your training."

"I'm not even sure how the hell I'll use it," I said, panic setting in.

Rhys gripped my shoulders. "You'll know when the moment is right. Trust yourself. Trust your wolf."

I thought about everything I'd learned from the men and women around me. At the heart of it was trust—in each other and ourselves.

I pulled air in through my nose and let it out through my mouth. I could do this.

Weapons clattered to the table, spilling out as Ender and Franco emptied duffel bags full of all types of gear. Ender looked around. "Bullets will do nothing to the mages. They need to be ended by blades. Try to decapitate or get a direct hit to the heart."

A muscle along Franco's jaw fluttered. "I'm ready for a little payback."

I was sure he was. The dark mages had nearly cost him his soul. Everyone kitted up, and I checked that Kingston's blade was still tucked into my waistband. I added a sword to my other side and a gun at my back, just in case.

As everyone readied themselves, I felt a wave of *something* pass through me. My gaze snapped to Hera. "The wards. They're down."

"Gods be with us," she whispered.

"We move now. Follow the paths we discussed," King ordered.

I felt voices in my head then, sweet caresses that had my eyes stinging.

"Love you to the ends of the earth, Birdie," Puck whispered through my mind.

"I'm with you every step," Brix vowed.

"Be safe, Kitten. May your blade strike true," Ender rasped.

"Know your strength," Locke said.

And, finally, there was Kingston. *"You're our true leader, Little Warrior. We'll follow you anywhere."*

Emotion clogged my throat as I sent only one message back. *"I love you more than I thought possible. We make it through together."*

We ran through the forest in our groupings, charging for the spot Rhys had seen in his mind. I ran beside Brix and King, our footsteps echoing one another's until the creatures stepped out from behind the trees.

Their robes swirled around them, pale faces almost glowing beneath the hoods, those haunting pure-white eyes tracking all of our movements. Something about those eyes reminded me of when Rhys's went white when he had a vision. What did that say about what the dark mages could sense in all of us?

I felt it then, the press of one of the mages on my mind, trying to get in. I slammed up my mental shields and bared my teeth at the group.

One dark mage stepped forward, and something about him seemed familiar. "Empath." He grinned as he raised a ball of smoke. "I can't wait to taste your power."

And then chaos erupted.

CHAPTER FIFTY

Wren

The mages were everywhere. Far more than we'd ever faced before, and they just kept coming, spilling out from around trees and across our borders.

Arrows whizzed through the air, and I knew Ender and Franco were on it. Mage after mage fell, but it didn't stop the rest of them.

"Prepare yourself, Little Empath," the familiar mage whispered in a tone that had ice filling my veins. "You're strong, but you're no match for me."

"You said that the last time," I snarled as I pulled my sword from its sheath.

The mage simply grinned, but it was as if he had no teeth at all. His smile was an absence of light and life. The chill running through me intensified.

You can do this. I chanted the words over and over in my mind as battle reigned around me. Brix and Kingston each fought three different dark mages, and I could see our other groupings fighting in the distance.

"There's no one to protect you now," the mage cooed. "Come to me willingly, and I'll make your end painless. I can even make it pleasurable." He waved his fingers in a come-hither motion with long fingernails the color of smoke.

My back teeth gnashed, and I took up a fighting stance. "I protect myself."

The dark mage didn't seem cowed by that. "As you wish. You'll watch all your beloveds and friends perish, simply because you wouldn't surrender."

As if to punctuate the point, a howl of pain sounded to my right as a ball of smoke hit Kingston's shoulder. He doubled over as pain rocked through him. But Brix swung out with two swords taking two mages' heads clean off.

Kingston's body rippled and he transformed on the spot, his wolf howling. I saw the injury closing before my eyes now that he'd shifted, but it would still zap some of his energy. The urge to protect them all was so strong. I wanted to shield them like I had that night at the gym when we were all attacked.

But I couldn't. There were too many of us, spread too far apart. All I could do was take out as many mages as possible.

A ball of smoke flew my way, and I ducked at the last possible second.

"Your mates make you weak," the mage snarled.

"No. They make me strong." I charged forward, my blade at the ready.

The mage blocked my first blow with magic, and I called on my caster half and the creek running mere feet away. Water from the stream rose and spun in the air. *Be with me, Mom.* I needed her now more than ever.

My caster gifts surged, splitting the arc of water into a dozen ropes. They circled the twelve mages' necks, cutting off their air supply until my pack mates took them down, one by one. All except the mage in front of me.

He tore the water rope off his neck, then charged forward and lashed out with a strike to my jaw. My hold on my caster magic wavered, and the water slammed back into the stream. But I didn't forget my lessons. This time, it was the training from Ender and King that I called on.

I used the force of the mage's blow to propel me into a roundhouse kick. My foot connected with the dark mage's jaw, making his head snap back. I lunged forward with my sword, ramming the blade straight into his chest.

But it hit just to the right of his heart.

The mage snapped and snarled, going almost feral as he ripped the sword from his chest. "What do you have now, Little Empath? Nothing."

He prowled toward me, and I reached for King's blade at my waist but came up empty. A curse slipped from my mouth. It must've slipped from my belt when the mage struck me. Now, I had nothing. The gun at the back of my belt would do nothing against this dark creature.

Rhys's voice filled my mind. *"Trust your wolf."*

The mage gripped my shoulders, his terrifying nails piercing my skin. "All that is yours will be mine."

I let my wolf free. But she didn't transform completely as I expected her to. Instead, I heard just one message in the space between her and I. *We banish him together.*

My hand shot out, my fingers lengthening to claws. I punched into the mage's chest. All my physical training coming together. My claws tightened around his heart, and I ripped it clean from his chest.

The mage stumbled back, his white eyes widening with shock. And then he fell.

It was as if all the other mages felt it, too. They howled in pain, clutching at their chests and beginning to fall. One by one, they tumbled to the ground, disappearing into nothing but a pile of robes.

My pack looked on in shock, so confused by the turn of events.

King jogged to my side in wolf form, his shoulder still oozing from his injury. *"He must've been their coven leader. End him, end them all."*

Relief swept through me. *"It's over."* I glanced down at him. *"We need to get you healed."*

A shout rang through my head as I moved to turn. Puck's voice rose. *"Wren! Watch out!"*

But it was too late. Some force hit me like a freight train, and then I was falling.

CHAPTER FIFTY-ONE

Puck

I WATCHED IN HORROR AS THE REDDISH WOLF WITH DEAD eyes took Wren to the ground, snapping and snarling. But worse, a black substance dripped from its teeth as it tried to get its jaws around her neck.

Kingston ripped into its hindquarter, making it howl as more wolves ran from the opposite side of the property. And I recognized some of them. *"Red River,"* I snarled through the pack link.

My shift came on instantly as I charged toward Wren, Brix, and King, but I heard Juan behind me. "Holy fuck," he cursed. "They're huge. And there are so many."

He was right. There were more than there should be.

"Mercenaries," Ender growled through our minds. *"I've seen some of them before. Hired guns with no loyalty."*

But I knew a healthy dose of Red River assholes was in the mix, too.

Wren just managed to escape the red wolf's clutches, grabbing for her sword that was now lying on the ground. She swiped at the wolf who looked like he was half demon, and everything in me seized.

Marcelle. It had to be. A shifter brought back from the dead by dark magic. Everything about him was pure evil. He might've had a shred of light in him before, but no longer. He was nothing but darkness now.

Rhys and Locke ran into the fray, guns at the ready, as Clara and her team rounded the other side in wolf form. I caught sight of Hera chanting some incantation I prayed would save our asses as Ender and Franco tried to take wolves out from their sniper's nest.

Marcelle snarled at Wren, that black, tar-like substance still dripping from his teeth. *"Going to make you pay."*

Everyone fighting on Arcane's side stilled. Because we could hear him. It shouldn't have been possible. The only beings that could hear one another were those joined by pack links or a completed mating bond. But whatever sick and twisted thing had been done to Marcelle had given him more gifts.

Brix leapt into the air, blade raised, coming down on Marcelle's back and aiming for his heart. But Marcelle turned at the last possible moment, batting Brix away as if he weighed nothing more than a twig. He hit a tree hard and slumped to the ground.

Wren cried out, trying to run for him, but Marcelle blocked her path. *"You won't escape me this time. I'll feel your blood dripping from my fangs before I let you go."*

I pushed harder, trying to make it to Wren, attempting to save her.

Wren lifted her blade. "Your cruelty makes you weak."

She struck out, but Marcelle ripped the blade from her hands with his teeth. Blood poured from his mouth, so dark it was nearly black. Wren leveled a kick at his head, shoving the blade farther into his mouth. Marcelle howled in pain.

One, two, three arrows pierced his hide, just as I reached him. Marcelle stumbled. My teeth sank into his neck, and the taste of his blood was foul on my tongue. Rotten. But I didn't let go. I shook the red wolf, feeling his neck snap, but I knew it wasn't enough. My teeth sank deeper until I felt his carotid artery. I clamped down on it and ripped it free.

Rhys raced forward, his hand punching into the red wolf from behind his shoulder blade, pulling his heart free.

"Give it to me," Hera yelled.

Rhys threw it toward her in some macabre game of catch, and Hera managed to snag it from the air, instantly beginning her chanting. A few moments later, the heart was engulfed in flames. She dropped it to the forest floor, breathing heavily. "He's dead. Now, he's really dead."

But it wasn't enough. There were still far too many wolves. The only one I didn't see was Bastian. The goddamned coward.

The inky black wolf I knew was Mei took on two mercenary wolves. One sank its teeth into her hindquarter, but Clara snarled in fury and pounced on him, snapping his neck.

Wren struggled to her feet as two wolves charged at her.

"You take the brown. I'll take the russet," Ender ordered.

I lunged at the brown one, raking my claws over its face as Wren stabbed it through the heart. Ender and Franco took down the second with arrows and bullets.

But it seemed as if it would never end. The invasion just kept coming. We were fighting them off, but we were struggling.

Locke leveled his weapon at a wolf about to lunge at Hera. He got off two shots before the whole world slowed.

I took in everything in the pauses between inhales and exhales. Bastian stepping out from between the trees. His claws lengthening. Those claws ripping across Locke's throat.

His eyes went wide with shock as he crumpled to the ground. And then he didn't move at all.

CHAPTER FIFTY-TWO

Wren

"Noooooo!" The word tore from my throat as Locke fell to the ground.

I was already running, not giving a damn if I was running toward the last person I should. I didn't care. All I cared about was getting to Locke. The purest soul of all of us.

Bastian laughed, the sound ugly and twisted. "You take from me, and I take from you, Little Flower. You should know that by now."

I sank to the ground, my spine jarring with the force of it. I rolled Locke to his back and put pressure on the wound. I poured all the energy I could through our bond. I gave him everything I had to give because I couldn't lose him.

"It's too late," Bastian rasped. "You'll never save him."

My mates raced toward us, but the moment they were steps away, they bounced off an invisible force field.

Bastian only laughed harder as they pounded against the ward.

"It'll never work. You see, those dark mages were none too pleased about you trying to break up their coven and killing some of their own. So, they came to me."

I gaped at my father as I pressed harder against Locke's throat, pouring more of my life's essence into him.

Bastian just grinned down at me. "We made a deal. I'd get you for a year, get an heir I can train to be a *true* leader, and they could have you for their little sacrifice after." He glanced around the forest. "Looks like they didn't fare too well. Pity. I guess I'll get to kill you myself in the end."

Snarls and howls lit the air as my mates tried in vain to get through the barrier. Hera was casting some sort of spell but coming up short. And I could only stare at the man who was supposed to be my father.

"You killed her, didn't you?" I croaked.

Bastian's face contorted. "Who?"

"My. Mother."

He sneered, his eyes darkening. "She *took* from me. Stole. Right out from under my nose. There's only one punishment for that. A lesson you'll soon learn. Again."

It wasn't that I hadn't known the truth deep in my heart, but hearing him say it aloud brought a kind of freedom. Knowing he'd admitted to the level of his cruelty.

"You're a monster," I whispered.

Bastian's grin was back. "You pay me such compliments, Little Flower. Now, yield."

Alpha vibes lit the air, pressing into me, trying to force my submission. But I wouldn't break. Sweat broke out across my brow as I tried to withstand Bastian's energy and keep Locke with me. "Don't you leave me," I murmured to Locke. "Stay."

"Yield!" Bastian bellowed. The force of his voice was a physical blow, and I rocked to the side.

Pain radiated through my skull and down my spine as I

struggled to stay upright. And then Rhys's voice filled my head. *"Use your gift, Little Empath."*

I blinked a few times, struggling to understand what he meant as enemy wolves surrounded us all, closing in with more numbers than we could ever hope to defeat. Snarls lit the air, and I knew I had no choice.

I lowered my shields and let the darkness in. Pain like nothing I'd ever known or felt before slammed into me as I took all the negative emotions inside. The cruelty, the quest for power, the bloodlust.

It was a living, breathing thing as I pulled it into me. Every ounce of it sent white-hot agony coursing through me. Spots danced in front of my vision, but through them, I saw our enemy wavering. Some of them looked confused, some stopped fighting altogether.

"What the hell are you doing?" Bastian demanded.

I pulled more, focusing on him, feeling the true depths of his depravity. "I'm stopping it," I croaked.

Bastian crossed the distance in three long strides and grabbed me by the neck, lifting me into the air. But that was a mistake. Because with the skin-to-skin contact, I could take more of that darkness. More of his evil.

"You hybrid abomination," he snarled, gripping me harder.

My air supply cut off, but I didn't stop. I pulled every ounce of darkness I felt. I took it all.

"Wren, stop!" Kingston yelled.

"Your nose is bleeding," Brix pleaded.

But I didn't stop. I *would* end this. I would snuff out every ounce of darkness. I would let in the light. Even if it cost me my life. I'd pay the price again and again if it meant the people I loved were safe.

My vision tunneled as Bastian squeezed harder, but I still kept taking.

"Her blood," Clara croaked. "It's black."

"She's taking all their darkness," Rhys whispered reverently.

The fighting had stopped. The only evil that remained was Bastian. If I could just take the last of his…

Then the light went out for good.

CHAPTER FIFTY-THREE

Kingston

IT WAS AS IF THE WHOLE WORLD SLOWED WITH THE HORROR of it. Locke's body lay unmoving on the ground, his skin far too pale, blood spilling out around him. Wren falling, falling, falling. She hit the forest floor with a deafening thud, that black blood still seeping out of her nose.

And Bastian just looked on in shock. As if he were truly horrified by what he'd done. The shield slipped as he spun around, trying to make sense of what he'd put into motion, but I didn't give a damn. I was already running, my brothers at my sides.

"Brix, Puck, take Locke. Ender, we've got Wren." My voice didn't even sound like my own. It was robotic and hollow. No feeling at all.

I dropped to my knees next to Wren. Her skin had gone pale, too. As if all the color that lived inside her had been sucked out. And then there was that damn black blood. All the darkness she'd taken from everyone around her.

"What have I done?" Bastian croaked.

Out of the corner of my eye, I saw him staring down at his hands, coming to terms with all the death and destruction he'd caused. All the pain, cruelty, the suffering he'd wrought.

His body seized, and he clutched at his chest. Clawing there. Henry, Clara's enforcer, moved Bastian as he hit the ground. His eyes went wide and then froze there, his body contorted. Henry pressed two fingers to his neck. "He's gone."

"Good riddance," Rhys spat.

I couldn't find it in me to care. I'd thought I would feel joy when Bastian's life ended, relief that the man who'd killed my sister's soul was finally gone. But I felt nothing.

"We need to move. Now," Ender growled.

I jerked my head in a nod. On three, Ender and I lifted Wren as Brix and Puck hoisted Locke. We moved through the forest as quickly as possible. Hera ran ahead, calling off a list of things she needed to Clara. Rhys, Juan, Franco, and the enforcers surrounded us, providing protection from people we no longer needed to be shielded from.

The still-standing members of the Red River pack, all the mercenaries. Confusion swept over their expressions, as well as grief and guilt. Some wept. Some wailed. Some simply looked shocked beyond comprehension.

Wren had given them true justice. To face the truth of what they'd done.

But I didn't give a damn about any of them. I didn't even give a damn about justice. I only cared about Wren and Locke.

"Hold them here," Hera ordered from up ahead. "Use the bond."

I focused on the tether that linked Wren and I for all eternity. The one that felt like the most beautiful chain. I pushed all the energy I could through that bond, and Wren let out a cough, more black blood seeping from her mouth.

"Fuck," Ender swore, so much grief and fear in his eyes.

"Don't," I clipped. "We're not losing her."

His gaze met mine. "We're not losing her."

Clyde and Dina stood holding open the back doors, their faces pale.

We charged in, getting Wren and Locke to the medical room as quickly as possible. Clara pulled out a second gurney from the corner. "Push them together," Hera ordered. "We need them close."

Clara moved instantly, shoving the beds together and locking them. We laid Locke and Wren gingerly on them as enforcers grabbed the ingredients that Hera called out. She muttered to herself as she mixed things. "I don't know if it'll be enough. They may be too far gone."

My heart lurched in my chest. "Please," I rasped. "Please, save them." They were the best of us. The kindest. The purest souls. This world would be so much darker without them in it. And my world would be black.

Hera cursed but began chanting over her bowl. Sparks swirled above it and then blinked out. She continued chanting as she poured the herbs over both their bodies. The sparks erupted again, illuminating every injury. Locke's were confined to his neck, but Wren's? They were everywhere.

Because the darkness was everywhere.

Hera stared at her as tears welled in her eyes. "It's not enough. My magic isn't enough."

I dropped to my knees beside the bed and pressed my lips to Wren's temple. "Don't leave me, Little Warrior. Fight. Please."

Rhys moved, tearing open cupboards in search of something.

"What the hell are you doing?" Hera barked.

"A syringe. I need a syringe."

Something in his voice spurred Hera into action. She moved to a drawer and pulled out a sealed packet.

Rhys took it quickly and ripped it open. Fastening the needle in place, he slid it into a vein on his forearm. As he pulled blood from his body, my eyes went wide. It wasn't red like you'd expect it to be. It was black, but with a shimmer that was hypnotizing.

Hera gasped, her gaze flying to Rhys's face. "You're a Nocturnae."

He quickly removed the needle and shoved the syringe into Hera's hand. "Give her my blood. It'll heal her."

Hera stood there for a moment, still frozen in shock.

"Now!" Rhys ordered. "Before it's too late."

That jerked Hera into motion. She moved to the side of the bed and plunged the needle into Wren's heart, injecting the blood directly. The moment it was in her system, you could see it. A glow began in her heart and spread like a wave of light throughout her body.

Sparks swam through her veins and through the air. One by one, the lights in the room flickered and then went out. And all we could do was let our hope light the darkness.

CHAPTER FIFTY-FOUR

Wren

I was flying. Completely weightless and soaring through the air. But everything was warm. Like a Caribbean sky. I never wanted to leave.

But there were voices. Some force trying to pull me back.

I frowned. I didn't want to go back. It was lovely here.

"Don't scowl at me, Birdie. You've been napping for long enough."

Birdie. Something about that tugged at me.

"Little Warrior, we need you," a deep, alpha voice called.

"He's right, Kitten. We're a mess without you."

Kitten.

My eyelids fluttered, and light pierced through that was almost too bright.

"There she is," Brix rasped.

It took me a second to put names with faces and for every part of me to come back to myself. I shot up on a gasp. "Locke!"

"Right here." He leaned into me, wrapping me in his arms.

I twisted in his hold, my fingers lifting to his neck to trace the scars there. "You're okay." Tears filled my eyes. "You're really okay?"

Locke dropped his forehead to mine. "I am. And so are you."

My tears fell faster. "I thought I'd lost you." I looked up as the rest of the guys climbed onto the bed, surrounding us. "I thought I'd lost all of you."

Puck kissed my temple. "Never, Birdie. I'm going to be giving you hell until we're old and gray."

"He's right," Brix said, weaving his fingers through mine. "You're stuck with us for eternity."

Ender's lips twitched. "She might be having second thoughts there."

A meow sounded, and Princess leapt onto the bed, squawking up a storm as she crawled up my body.

One corner of Kingston's mouth kicked up. "She's been worried about you, too."

I cuddled her to my chest. "Missed you, too." I looked up at the guys. "What happened?"

They all shared a look, and dread pooled in my stomach.

"What?" I pressed.

Kingston laid a hand over my thigh, squeezing. "You took all the dark emotions from Red River and their mercenaries."

Memories came back in flashes. Bastian slicing Locke's throat and locking us behind wards. Admitting that he'd killed my mother. Telling me what he had planned for me.

"Rhys," I whispered. "His voice was in my head. Telling me to use my empathic gifts."

"Idiot," Ender muttered.

Puck smacked his shoulder. "Well, he saved our asses twice, so maybe no name-calling."

"What happened to Red River?" I asked.

Brix traced the shape of my tattoo through the blankets

because he'd memorized every line. "It's like you took all the badness from them. It left them to face what they'd done."

"That's the ultimate justice. Knowing all the harm you've caused and truly feeling it," King rasped.

I looked at him. "Bastian?"

I wasn't sure what I was hoping to hear. That he was dead? Jailed?

Kingston gripped my thigh tighter. "He's gone, Wren. He'd done so much evil, his mind couldn't process it. He had a heart attack."

A phantom pressure bore down on my chest. The weight of so much heartache and pain. But as all my mates touched me, bringing their comfort, the pressure lifted as quickly as it came.

"Balance," I whispered.

Locke's brows pulled together. "What do you mean?"

"It's something Hera told me. Our world needs balance, magic requires it. For balance to be restored, he needed to be taken."

Locke's lips brushed the side of my face. "We love you."

"And I love you." I looked around the room. "How's everyone else?"

"Just fine," Brix assured me.

"And being annoying," Ender muttered. "They won't leave until they've laid eyes on you."

I laughed. "Too much peopling for you?"

"Far too much," he griped.

My brow furrowed. "Rhys, you said he saved us twice. What was the other time?"

The room went completely quiet, and that dread returned to my belly.

"What happened?"

"He saved your life," Kingston whispered.

I tried to search my mind for a memory of the time after I fell to the ground, but there was nothing. "How?" I asked.

Brix looked at Ender, who nodded. "Rhys gave you some of his blood."

My frown deepened. I knew vampire blood had healing properties, but it wasn't all that much stronger than the magic Hera could do. "Is Hera all right? Was she hurt?" It was the only reason I could think of for her not healing me.

Kingston shook his head. "She's fine. But your injuries...they were more than she could handle."

Ender gripped my foot through the blankets, his thumbs digging into the arch. "Rhys isn't just a vampire. He's a Nocturnae."

My jaw went slack. I'd only heard the term a handful of times. Nocturnae were what vampires came from. An ancient race with gifts that were whispered about but never known for sure. It was said they'd lived for most of their lives in another dimension. And if our supernatural world here on Earth got word that one was in our midst...

My eyes burned. "He risked everything for me." I was already throwing off the covers and rising from the bed. "I have to thank him."

"He's gone." There was such sadness in Ender's voice. "He left the night after the battle without saying a word."

An ache took root in my chest. "He's all alone," I whispered.

Ender's gaze collided with mine. "He wants it that way."

I shook my head. "He needs someone."

"I know. But he has to make that choice," Ender said.

Kingston pushed to his feet and wrapped me in a hug. "We'll find a way to thank him. But for now, the rest of your friends—your *family*—want to see you."

Those words were the best balm. I quickly showered with a spot from Brix to make sure I was steady. Puck blow-dried my hair while Locke picked out my comfiest sweats. King and Ender helped me dress. And then we were heading downstairs.

The sound of laughter and voices came from the kitchen, and

those were a balm, too. I let them wrap around me as I moved toward them. When I stepped into the space, all talking ceased.

Clyde was out of his chair first, ambling toward me and pulling me into a hug. "Girlie."

"I'm good." My throat clogged with emotion, making it hard for the words to escape.

"Don't you ever do that to me again," he whispered hoarsely.

"Damn straight," Dina said. "You know I've got a bat, and I'm not afraid to use it."

A choked laugh bubbled out of me.

"You don't want to cross her, Wren," Franco called.

Juan let out an exaggerated shiver. "She scares me."

Clara stood from where she was cuddled with Hera on a window seat and crossed to me. She cupped my cheek as Clyde released me. "Truly worthy of the name your men have given you, Little Warrior." She tipped her head to mine, the ultimate show of respect from an alpha.

"Clara," I choked out.

"Honored to have you as a sister."

"Beyond honored." My gaze moved to Hera. "Thank you. For everything you have done." That gaze trailed over everyone in the room. "All of you. You are truly the greatest gifts I've ever been given."

EPILOGUE

Wren

FIVE YEARS LATER

The warm spring wind lifted my hair as I looked out from the stage to the crowd below. So many happy faces framed by the stunning landscape of the Colorado campus. Almost everyone was in attendance, and that was the greatest gift of all. The only thing that would've made it better was if Rhys had been here, too.

It had been a hard five years of accelerated coursework and in-practice training, but it had all been worth it because I had found my calling. The place where my supernatural and human halves could come together in service of others.

And I'd made it through the long hours of studying, my internship, and endless tests because of all the amazing people in the audience today. My gaze tracked over the three rows they took up close to the front.

Clyde and Dina sat together, their hands clasped, smiles beaming. They'd finally gotten married last year, and we'd had the party of all parties to celebrate. Next to them was Franco and his wife, Marilee. He bounced their two-year-old boy on his knee as he giggled. Juan was next to them, his hand in Mei's. Not long after the battle, the two of them had realized they were mates, and his inappropriate jokes were now cast only in her direction.

In the row behind them was the one friend I'd managed to make before coming to Crescent Creek, Hayden. She beamed up at me with such pride and happiness. When her eyes began to fill, one of her mates, Cillian, pulled her against him and kissed her hair. Hayden's four other mates looked on in a mix of worry and thinking she was adorable. And, gods, it was good to have my friend fully back in my life.

In the third row of family was Hera, who cuddled a baby girl to her chest as Clara kissed her temple. Their other mates hadn't been able to make the trek from the UK, but Puck's parents had. All of them looked on with such joy in their faces. Helping Puck find his family again was just another gift in my embarrassment of riches.

And finally, my men. They looked devastating in their suits, wearing their pride like accessories. Kingston's ice-blue eyes shone, picking up the undertones of his shirt. *"Love you,"* he spoke into my mind.

Puck shot me a grin that had my belly warming. *"What do you have on under that robe, Birdie?"*

It took everything in me not to laugh.

"You would make things dirty," Locke said exasperatedly.

I fingered the lock necklace at my throat, feeling the bond between us all.

"Kitten can take it. Can't you, Dr. Arcane?" Ender challenged.

When we'd had our mating ceremony a few months after the battle, we'd all chosen our pack name as our last name, truly binding us together as one.

"You make us so proud, Little Warrior." Brix's eyes glittered like

gemstones. *"You're going to help so many people find their way through the dark."*

Those words coming from Brix meant something more, knowing the darkness he and I had weathered together. *"Don't you dare make me cry."*

"Show-off," Puck muttered.

The rest of the guys just laughed.

The names continued to be called out as they worked through our small class in reverse alphabetical order. The dean turned her gaze to me, a smile on her lips. "Our last graduate is incredibly special. She's not only graduating at the top of her class, but she also created a mental health clinic to serve her community, free of charge. She's someone who never gives up the fight when it comes to her patients, and our world is a better place because she's in it. Wren Arcane."

As I stood, I heard my mother's voice in my head. *"So proud of you, my little Wren."*

My eyes filled with the happiest of tears as I crossed the stage and shook the dean's hand. She gave me a hug and my diploma, and I kept right on moving. As my classmates threw their caps into the air, I only had eyes for my mates.

I hurried down the stairs and through the throng of people that had erupted, but my men were already on their feet and on their way to me. Just like always.

Puck hoisted me into the air, spinning me around. "My beautiful Birdie."

As he lowered me, Brix kissed one temple and Locke the other. King took my mouth, and Ender wrapped his arms around me from behind. I was sure there were people in the audience who thought it odd, but I didn't give a damn. Because I was happy. And now, I was going to give my mates the same happiness.

"There's something I want to tell you," I croaked.

All my mates stilled, waiting.

Closing my eyes for a moment, I let my scent shields drop.

The same ones that had hidden my shifter and caster natures had been hiding something else.

King's nostrils flared as he scented. "Pregnant?"

Ender's hand palmed my belly. "Pups?"

"Yes," I breathed, my eyes going to Brix to read his reaction.

His fingers slid through mine, squeezing. "Never been happier."

Locke's lips brushed across mine. "Best gift we've ever received."

A grin split Puck's face as he turned to his family and shouted, "I'm gonna be a dad!"

I couldn't hold in my laughter as happy tears streamed down my face. Because we truly had everything. And that would never end.

Curious about Rhys? Get his story in the Blood Bound series.

Want to know more about Hayden and her dragon shifter mates? Get their story in *Twilight of Embers,* book one in The Dragons of Ember Hollow series.

READ ON FOR A SNEAK PEEK AT RHYS'S STORY, STARTING IN

Rhys

I'D MADE PEACE WITH THE RAGE THAT LIVED INSIDE ME. IT MIGHT seem odd that rage and peace could coexist, but that was where the numbness entered. If fury lived inside you for long enough, you got used to its burn and it sort of became background noise.

Not today, though.

Not when Pax had called me here. To her.

It had all the memories flooding back. My hand moved to the scar on my chest on instinct, feeling the raised flesh. The demon mark. Getting her to safety had cost me nearly everything. And it seemed this fated bond wasn't done taking from me.

I gritted my teeth as I drove my Aston Martin DB12 through the streets of Boston. Human cities were not for me. There was too much noise. Pollution. Chaos. I preferred the wide-open spaces you could find elsewhere. I'd lived in Montana, Alaska, Maine, Washington, and countless other places where I could find fresh air at least, but none of them were home.

My mouth curved the barest amount when I thought about how Soraya was seeking out her version of home. Boston was only about an hour from Salem, the city that was home to the descendants of her kind. Just as Nocturnae were vampires' ancestors, witches descended from Luminaries. If they only knew how much Luminaries despised the term—to them witches were merely less powerful versions of what they were meant to be.

It was as if some invisible tether had called Soraya here, to the closest to home she could get. A scowl twisted my lips. Even that could prove dangerous if the wrong people somehow put two and two together. We'd already had to move her once—not that she knew it.

I shifted in my seat, struggling to get comfortable. But I never was.

I made the hour-long drive to the small town outside of Boston. Normally, the farther I got from those crowded human streets, the more my tension eased. But not today. Today, each mile that passed wound my muscles tighter until I was pretty sure my jaw had a new hairline fracture.

It would heal.

As I wound my way through the picturesque neighborhoods, the properties slowly got larger and larger. When Pax informed me that Soraya was moving out of Boston, I'd put him up in a house that would provide privacy. Someplace close, but not too close.

Slowing at the gate, I rolled down my window and plugged in the code. In a matter of minutes, I was pulling up to the home on the estate. With eight bedrooms and ten bathrooms, I wasn't sure what Pax was utilizing it all for, but at least we had room to talk.

I climbed out of my rental car and slammed the door. As I started up the steps, Pax appeared in the entryway.

"How was the trip?" he asked.

I glared at him as I reached the top stair. "How do you think? I don't do well with being beckoned."

Pax winced. He rarely demanded things of me. I could think of only twice before in our 160-year friendship. But he was now.

"It's time," he said softly.

Every thread of tension inside me wound impossibly tighter. I refused to believe that was the case. Fifteen years wasn't nearly long enough. But who was I kidding? Endless centuries wouldn't have been enough.

"Not yet," I growled.

Pax sighed, opening the door wider and ushering me in. He walked through the echoey hallway, guiding us into a massive kitchen. It was bright. Too bright. Living in the dark for my entire life, I still hadn't gotten used to the days in the human realm.

"Blood?" Pax asked.

He'd likely been living on bagged human blood, but that wouldn't do for me. For so many reasons. Instead, I'd been forced to live on the animal stuff.

I shook my head and waited.

Pax gripped the edge of the counter. "She's getting sick. It's time. She needs to go home."

Panic burned through me, its heat different than rage. This burned hotter, leaving scars in its wake. "What do you mean, sick?"

He grimaced. He'd never particularly enjoyed giving me bad news. "The headaches are getting worse. One took her down last night for six hours. If we leave her here for much longer, I fear it could do permanent damage."

A battle waged within me: the fated bond versus my hatred. The bond rode me hard, wanting to fix things for her, protect her, heal her. It was the way mating bonds worked. They made you care for your fated. But my hatred for her people—for her family—pushed back against it, fighting to burn the bond to ashes.

But it was also more than that. If we brought her back to Lumaria, our enemies would be everywhere. Once the truth was revealed and they found out we were fated, no one would be on our side. Her people. Mine. Every other Nocturnae House would worry that it might mean an alliance between the House of Firelight and the Luminaries. And I couldn't forget the demons. They knew she had power within her—a power they wanted.

"You need to see her," Pax said softly.

"No." The single word cracked through the air like a whip.

Since that day, I'd done everything I could not to see her. Olympia had bound her magic and mind, so when she entered the human realm, Soraya wouldn't remember her past or her magic. Pax had placed her with a human family I'd vetted and he continued to watch over her—but he had been the only one with her, the invisible guard making sure she was safe until she was old enough for him to use a cloaking spell to look the right age to be one of her classmates.

"It's time," he pressed, albeit gently. "You can only fight this for so long. It will drain you and her."

My back teeth ground together because I knew he was right. You couldn't break a bond without it ending in death or madness because souls were linked.

I'd tried to find other options. I'd spent countless hours of my purgatory here in the human realm researching. Because it wasn't like I could return home. Not when there was a price on my head.

But that's what happened when you kidnapped the Luminary Prince's promised one.

"I can bring you with me today, introduce you as my cousin or something," Pax went on.

I scowled. "We look nothing alike."

Pax rolled his eyes. "Cousins by marriage, maybe? She won't question it. She doesn't look for enemies and traitors around every corner."

Unlike you.

I heard the unspoken words but took no offense. If anything, I worried that Soraya didn't look for those enemies and traitors because she'd have to start. The people of Lumaria would see one of two things when they looked at her: either an abomination—something that went against the gods—or a source of power they wanted to tap.

Neither was good.

I couldn't even count on my own brother. In the few hours I'd had before escaping with Soraya to stash her in the human world, I'd confided in Ayden. How else could I prepare him to protect our kingdom in my absence? To say he hadn't been supportive was an understatement.

"And then what? We'll have tea and tell her she's from an ancient, magical race and that I'm her fated mate?" Even just saying the words made me sick.

"She's kind, Rhys. She's got a heart of gold. And she's funny. You'll like her."

A storm swirled within me as a new wave of fury swept through me. "Have. You. Touched. Her?"

Pax stumbled back, his eyes going wide. "What? Are you mad? She's your fated. I would never. And you know she's not my type."

The red tinge to my vision eased a fraction as I tried to regain control. I absently noticed that I'd cracked the edge of the island's marble when I gripped it.

Jealous fury.

I was never jealous. But Pax had been in her life nearly every day. At first, watching from afar, and then inserting himself into her life in high school—a built-in best friend for everything she needed. He knew her better than anyone.

"Sorry," I rasped.

Relief swept across his expression. "It's okay. I get it. She's your fated. Emotions are bound to run high."

But I couldn't afford any of them. I would not allow myself to care for this…Luminary. My lip curled just thinking the word.

Yes, I was bound to her. There was nothing I could do to change that. So I would protect her. But I would never love her.

On a station platform, with nothing to read,
and a four-hour train journey stretching ahead of him...

That's where the story began for Penguin founder Allen Lane. With only 'shabby reprints of shoddy novels' on offer, he resolved to make better books for readers everywhere.

By the time his train pulled into London, the idea was formed. He would bring the best writing, in stylish and affordable formats, to everyone. His books would be sold in bookstores, stationers and tobacconists, for no more than the price of a ten-pack of cigarettes.

And on every book would be a Penguin, a bird with a certain 'dignified flippancy', and a friendly invitation to anyone who wished to spend their time reading.

In 1935, the first ten Penguin paperbacks were published. Just a year later, three million Penguins had made their way onto our shelves.

Reading was changed forever.

—

A lot has changed since 1935, including Penguin, but in the most important ways we're still the same. We still believe that books and reading are for everyone. And we still believe that whether you're seeking an afternoon's escape, a vigorous debate or a soothing bedtime story, all possibilities open with a book.

Whoever you are, whatever you're looking for,
you can find it with Penguin.